Robert Williams Buchanan

Ballad Stories of the Affections

Robert Williams Buchanan

Ballad Stories of the Affections

ISBN/EAN: 9783744782050

Printed in Europe, USA, Canada, Australia, Japan

Cover: Foto ©Andreas Hilbeck / pixelio.de

More available books at **www.hansebooks.com**

BALLAD STORIES.

BALLAD STORIES

OF THE

AFFECTIONS.

𝔉rom the 𝔖candinabian.

BY

ROBERT BUCHANAN.

ADAM OEHLENSCHLAEGER.

LONDON:

SAMPSON LOW, SON, AND MARSTON,

CROWN BUILDINGS, 188 FLEET STREET.

1869.

TRANSLATOR'S PREFACE.

RANSMITTED, in the same manner as the Scottish and Breton ballads, as a precious heritage from father to son, the old ballads of Scandinavia were preserved by popular recitation. With all their contradictions and inconsistencies, they are national—no ballads more so—distinguishable in genius from the Scottish writings of the same class, although possessing many delicate points of similarity. As for the themes, some are of German and others of Southern origin, while many are chiefly Scandinavian. The adventurers who swept southward long ago, to range themselves under the banners of strange chiefs, not seldom returned home brimful of wild exaggerated stories, to beguile many a winter night; and these stories in course of time became so imbedded in popular tradition, that it was difficult to guess whence they primarily came, and gathered

so much moss of the soil in the process of rolling
down the years, that their foreign colour soon faded
into the sombre greys of Northern poesy. Travellers
flocking northward in the middle ages added to the
stock, bringing subtle delicacies from Germany, and
fervid tendernesses from Italy and Spain. But much
emanated from the North itself—from the storm-tost
shores of Denmark, and from the wild realm of the
eternal snow and midnight sun. There were heroes
and giants breasting the Dovre Fjord, as well as
striding over the Adriatic. Certain shapes there
were which loved the sea-surrounded little nation
only. The Lindorm, hugest of serpents, crawled
near Verona; but the Valrafn, or Raven of Battle,
loved the swell and roar of the fierce North Sea.
The Dragon ranged as far south as Syria; but the
Ocean-sprite liked cold waters, and flashed, icy-
bearded, through the rack and cloud of storm. In
the Scottish ballad we find the Kelpie, but search in
vain for the Mermaid. In the Breton ballad we see
the "Korrigaun," seated with wild eyes by the side
of the wayside well, but hear little of the mountain-
loving Trolds and Elves. It is in supernatural con-
ceptions indeed, in the creation of typical spirits to
represent certain ever-present operations of Nature,

that the Danish ballads excel—being equalled in that respect only by the German *Lieder*, with which they have so very much in common. They seldom or never quite reach the rugged force of *language* shown in such Breton pieces as "Jannedik Flamm" and the wild early battle-song. They are never so refinedly tender as the best Scottish pieces. We have to search in them in vain for the exquisite melody of the last portion of "Fair Annie of Loch-ryan," or for the pathetic and picturesque loveliness of "Clerk Saunders," in those exquisite lines *after the murder*—

> " Clerk Saunders he started, and Margaret she turned
>   Into his arms, as asleep she lay;
> And sad and silent was the night
>   That was between thir twae.
>
> " And they lay still, and sleepèd sound,
>   Until the day began to daw.
> As kindly to him she did say,
>   ' It's time, true love, ye were awa'!'
>
> " But he lay still and sleepèd sound,
>   Albeit the sun began to sheen;
> She looked atween her and the wa',
>   And dull and drowsy were his een."

But they have a truth and force of their own which stamp them as genuine poetry. In the mass, they might be described as a rough compromise of language with painfully vivid imagination. Nothing can be finer than the stories they contain, or more dramatic than the situations these stories entail; but no attempt is made to polish the expression or refine the imagery. They give one an impression of intense earnestness—of a habit of mind at once reticent and shadowed with the strangest mysteries. That the teller believes heart and soul in the tale he is going to tell, is again and again proved by his dashing, at the very beginning of his narrative, into the catastrophe—

> " It was the young Herr Haagen,
> He lost his sweet young life ! "

And all because he would not listen to the warnings of a mermaid, but deliberately cut her head off. There is no such pausing, no such description, as would infer a doubt of the reality of any folk in the story. The point is, not to convey the fact that sea-maidens exist, a truth of which every listener is aware, but to prove the folly of disregarding their advice when they warn us against going to sea in bad weather.

The region to which we are introduced being that

of tradition, not of history, we must have plenty of faith if we wish to be happy there. Everything we see is colossal, things as well as men being fashioned on a mighty scale : the adventurous nature burns fierce as fire, lives fall thickly as leaves in harvest, and the heroes sweep hither and thither, strong as the sword-blow, bright as the sword-flash. Two powers exist—physical strength and the command of the supernatural. Again and again, however, we leave the battle-field, and come upon "places of nestling green," where dwell those gentler emotions which belong to all time and are universal. We have love-making, ploughing and tilling, drinking and singing. At every step we meet a beautiful maiden, frequently unfortunate, generally in love, and invariably with golden hair.

Among the pieces founded on popular superstition, appear, as has been suggested, many of the gems of Danish ballad literature. In nearly every one of them we hear of enchantment, of men and maidens transformed into strange shapes ; and it is remarkable that the worker of the foul witchcraft is invariably a cruel *stepmother*. The best of them are terse and strong, and impress us more solemnly than do the " Battle Ballads." We are in a strange region, as we read;—and everywhere around us rises the wail of people who are doomed to visit the scenes of their humanity in unnatural forms.

> "*In nova fert Animus mutatas dicere formas*
> *Corpora*,"

might be the motto of any future translator of these pieces. How the Bear of Dalby turned out to be a King's son; how Werner the Raven, through drinking the blood of a little child, changed into the fairest knight the eye of man could see; how an ugly serpent changed in the same way, and all by means of a pretty kiss from fair little Signe. But there are other and finer kinds of supernatural manifestation. The Elves flit on "Elfer Hill," and slay the young men; they dance in the grove by moonlight, and the daughter of the Elf King sends Herr Oluf home, a dying man, to his bride. The ballad in which the latter event occurs, bears, by the way, a striking resemblance to the Breton ballad of the "Korrigaun." The dead rise. A corpse accosts a horseman who is resting by a well, and makes him swear to avenge his death; and, late at night, tormented by the sin of having robbed two fatherless bairns, rides a weary ghost; the refrain concerning whom has been reported verbatim, for no earthly purpose, by Longfellow, in his "Saga of King Oluf :"—

" Dead rides Sir Morten of Foglesong !"

The Trolds of the mountain besiege a peasant's house, and the least of them all insists on having the peasant's wife ; but the catastrophe is a transformation—a prince's son. "The Deceitful Merman" beguiles Marstig's daughter to her death, and the piece in which he does so is interesting as being the original of Goethe's "Fisher."* Another ballad, " Agnete and the Merman," begins—

> " On the high tower Agnete is pacing slow,
> Sudden a Merman upsprings from below,
> Ho ! ho ! ho !
> A Merman upsprings from the water below !"

"Agnete ! Agnete !" he cries, "wilt thou be my true-love—my all-dearest ?" " Yea, if thou takest me with thee to the bottom of the sea." They dwell together eight years, and have seven sons. One day, Agnete, as she sits singing under the blue water, " hears the clocks of England clang," and straightway

---

* Goethe found the poem translated in Herder's " Volks-lieder."

asks and receives permission to go on shore to church. She meets her mother at the church-door. "Where hast thou been these eight years, my daughter?" "I have been at the bottom of the sea," replies Agnete, "and have seven sons by the Merman." The Merman follows her into the church, and all the small images turn away their eyes from him. "Hearken, Agnete! thy small bairns are crying for thee." "Let them cry as long as they will;—I shall not return to them." And the cruel one cannot be persuaded to go back. This pathetic story, so capable of poetic treatment, has been exquisitely paraphrased by Oehlenschläger, whose poem I have here translated in preference to the original. The Danish Mermen, by the way, seem to have been good fellows, and badly used. One Rosmer Harmand does many kindly acts, but is rewarded with base ingratitude by everybody. The tale of Rosmer bears a close resemblance to the romance of Childe Rowland, quoted by Edgar in "Lear."

Of the large mass of ballads dealing with ordinary sorrows and joys consequent on the domestic affections, it is unnecessary to offer any description, since they form the bulk of the pieces here printed.* The

* Udvalgte Danske viser fra Middelalderen, efter A. S.

longest and best of them all is " Axel and Walborg."
This exquisite poem has been for centuries popular
over all Scandinavia; places innumerable claim the
honour of possessing Walborg's grave, and rude pic-
tures of the hapless lovers are scattered far and wide
among the cottages of the North. As a picture of
manners and customs alone, the ballad is priceless.
Note, for example, the ecclesiastic ceremony, wherein
the rascally Prince Hogen plays so black a part.

In addition to a selection of old ballads, I have
given, for the sake of variety, a few modern pieces,
by Oehlenschläger and others. Out of the numerous
originals, I have selected for the present purpose
those which seemed the purest and best, passing
over with reluctance several fine specimens which
had been well rendered by previous translators. My

Vedels og P. Syvs trykte Udgaver og efter Laandskrevne
Samlinger udgivne paa ny af Abrahamson, Myerup, og
Rahbek. (Copenhagen, 1812.) Such is the title of the
work from which most of the antique ballads here translated
have been taken; but numerous other collections—Swedish,
Norwegian, and Danish—have been referred to and used.
The modern pieces by Oehlenschläger are to be found among
his collected poems, in the editions published at Copenhagen.
Those by Hoëdt and Bögh are taken from a little miscellan-
eous collection of verse, edited by Ingemann, and picked up
by me for a trifle at a Danish bookstall.—R. B.

task, on the whole, has been one of no ordinary anxiety. Next to the difficulty of writing a good ballad ranks the difficulty of translating a good ballad, and very few men have succeeded in doing either. Had I consulted my own taste, and translated throughout in broad old Scotch (the only really fitting equivalent for old Danish), I should not only have hopelessly bewildered English readers, but have laid my efforts open to dangerous comparison with those of Jamieson.* I have, therefore, done the best I could in the English dialect, using Scotch words liberally, but only such Scotch words as are quite familiar to all readers of our own ballads.

R. B.

---

* Robert Jamieson, who, among his "popular ballads," published in 1806, gave five from the Danish, rendered with a rugged picturesqueness transcending the best efforts in that direction of Scott himself. This Jamieson was a veritable singer, and struck some fine chords from a Scotch harp of his own.

CONTENTS.

INDUCTION: THE SUNKEN CITY.

WHERE the sea is smiling
   So blue and cold,
There stood a city
   In days of old;
But the black earth opened
   To make a grave,
And the city slumbers
   Beneath the wave.

Where life and beauty
   Dwelt long ago,
The oozy rushes
   And seaweeds grow;
And no one sees,
   And no one hears,
And none remember
   The far-off years.

But go there, lonely,
    At eventide,
And hearken, hearken
    To the lisping tide;
And faint sweet music
    Will float to thee,
Like church bells chiming
    Across the sea.

It is the olden,
    The sunken town,
Which faintly murmurs
    Far fathoms down;
Like the sea-winds breathing
    It murmurs by,
And the sweet notes tremble,
    And sink, and die.

Where now is moorland,
    All dark and dry,
Where fog and night-mist
    For ever lie,

Of old there blossomed,
   Divinely free,
A flowery kingdom
   Of Poesy.

A wondrous region
   Of visions proud,
'Neath bright blue heaven
   And white dream-cloud !
With scent of roses,
   And song of birds,
And gentle zephyrs
   Of loving words.

Each thing of beauty
   The old earth bore,
Each tone, each odour,
   (Alas ! no more !)
By Art and Music
   Were hither brought,
And grew eternal
   In divinest thought.

Here lies the moorland,
　　All dark and dry,
Here fogs and night-mist
　　For ever lie ;
And no one sees,
　　And no one hears,
And few remember
　　These far-off years.

But if thou hast not
　　In sin and strife
Forgot already
　　Thy childish life,
If things that harden
　　The human heart
Have not yet murdered
　　Thy nobler part—

Then on that moorland,
　　In the summer dark,
While the wind sighs past thee,
　　Stand still and hark,

And a faint sweet music
   Will float to thee,
Like church bells chiming
   Across the sea.

It is the world
   That once hath been,
Which sadly chimeth,
   Itself unseen ;
Like the sea-winds breathing.
   The tones creep by—
They faint, they tremble,
   And sweetly die !

EVEN-SONG.

SAFE in its earth nest lying,
  The bird is closing its eyes :
Dream !—while the wind is flying
  From its lair in the lofty skies !
Sweet in its earth nest lying,
  The flower is sinking to sleep :
Dream !—while the waves are crying
  On shores of the mighty deep !

For, dearest, thine eyelid closes,
  Safe as the bird's in the bower ;
Thy golden brow reposes,
  Sweet as the head of the flower.
Night wind, murmur yonder !
  Sea-wave, break and scream !
Your voices can never wander
  To the beautiful shores of Dream !

SIGNELIL THE SERVING-MAIDEN.

THE lady spake to Signelil,
  "*Signelil, my maiden!*
Wherefore, wherefore so thin and ill?"
  But the sorrow stings so sorely!

Sma' wonder I am sae ill and thin.
  Malfred, O my lady!
I hae sae muckle to sew and spin."
  But the sorrow stings so sorely!

"Before, thy cheek was rosy red.
  Signelil, my maiden!
Now 'tis pale as the cheek o' the dead."
  But the sorrow stings so sorely!

"I can nae longer hide ought frae thee,
  Malfred, O my lady!
Thy son hath plighted his vows to me."
  But the sorrow stings so sorely!

" My son hath plighted his troth to thee,
    Signelil, my maiden !
Say, what gifts did he dare to gie ? "
    But the sorrow stings so sorely !

" He gave me the silver buckled shoon,
    Malfred, O my lady !
I wear when tramping up and doon.
    But the sorrow stings so sorely !

" He gave to me the silken sark,
    Malfred, O my lady !
'Tis slit and torn wi' my weary wark.
    But the sorrow stings so sorely !

" On my finger he put a gold ring fine,
    Malfred, O my lady !
As bonnie as glitters on fingers o' thine."
    But the sorrow stings so sorely !

" What matters the gifts he dared to gie,
    Signelil, my maiden !
Since he never can be wed to thee ? "
    But the sorrow stings so sorely !

" Yea, he hath sworn to marry me,
  Malfred, O my lady !
Gifts he gave as to ony ladie."
  But the sorrow stings so sorely !

" What mattereth the oaths he swore,
  Signelil, my maiden !
Many a lass hath heard them before."
  But the sorrow stings so sorely !

" I hae the gift o' minstrelsie,
  Malfred, O my lady !
Nae man can hear wi' a tearless e'e.
  But the sorrow stings so sorely !

" Whene'er I take my harp on my knee,
  Malfred, O my lady !
Thy son must show he loveth me."
  But the sorrow stings so sorely !

She touched the string, she sang o' love,
  Signelil the maiden !
The young knight heard in the room above.
  But the sorrow stings so sorely !

Unto his little foot-page cried he,
  " Fetch Signelil the maiden !
Bid her quickly come hither to me !"
  But the sorrow stings so sorely !

Upon the cushioned couch slapped he :
  " Signelil, my maiden !
Sit down, dear love, and play to me !
  But the sorrow stings so sorely !

" Hast thou not kissed me tenderlie ?
  Signelil, my maiden !
Dost thou not keep the gifts I gie ?
  But the sorrow stings so sorely !

" Thou art my dearest, thou art my bride,
  Signelil, my maiden !
Thou shalt sit, thou shalt sleep, full soon at my
    side."
  But the sorrow stings so sorely !

Signelil is her lord's ladie !
  Signelil the maiden !
She won him with love and with minstrelsie.
  But the sorrow stings so sorely !

THE SOLDIER.

 SAW him at morning adown the green glen,
    Young, bonnie, and merry, a man among
    men ;
There sang he aloud with the birds, as he passed,
So merry a ditty—ah me ! 'twas the last !

I saw him at noon by the side of the stream,—
There walked we together, and talked in a dream :
He kissed me, he kissed me, and, clasping me fast,
Sighed, "Maybe, belovèd, this kiss is the last ! "

I saw him when gloaming was gathering gray,
Pale, pale, on the greensward, smit sore in the fray ;
One look on my face he in silence upcast,
And bade me farewell with a smile—with the last !

And since, when 'tis dark over meadow and stream,
I have seen him a thousand times over in dream,
And first have sighed low to the spirit who passed,
That he was the first one, and would be the last !

THE CHILDREN IN THE MOON.

HEARKEN, child, unto a story!
  For the moon is in the sky,
And across her shield of silver,
  See! two tiny cloudlets fly.

Watch them closely, mark them sharply,
  As across the light they pass,—
Seem they not to have the figures
  Of a little lad and lass?

See, my child, across their shoulders
  Lies a little pole; and, lo!
Yonder speck is just the bucket,
  Swinging softly to and fro.

It is said, these little children,
  Many and many a summer night,
To a little well far northward
  Wandered in the still moonlight.

To the wayside well they trotted,
  Filled their little buckets there,
And the Moon-man, looking downward,
  Saw how beautiful they were.

Quoth the man, " How vexed and sulky
  Looks the little rosy boy !
But the little handsome maiden   .
  Trips behind him full of joy.

" To the well behind the hedgerow
  Trot the little lad and maiden ;
From the well behind the hedgerow
  Now the little pail is laden.

" How they please me ! how they tempt me !
  Shall I snatch them up to-night ?
Snatch them, set them here for ever
  In the middle of my light ?

" Children, aye, and children's children,
  Should behold my babes on high,
And my babes should smile for ever,
  Calling others to the sky ! "

Thus the philosophic Moon-man
　　Muttered many years ago,
Set the babes with pole and bucket,
　　To delight the folks below.

Never is the bucket empty,
　　Never are the children old ;
Ever when the moon is shining
　　We the children may behold.

Ever young and ever little,
　　Ever sweet and ever fair !
When thou art a man, my darling.
　　Still the children will be there !

Ever young and ever little,
　　They will smile when thou art old ;
When thy locks are thin and silver,
　　Theirs will still be shining gold.

They will haunt thee from their heaven,
　　Softly beckoning down the gloom—
Smiling in eternal sweetness
　　On thy cradle, on thy tomb !

HELGA AND HILDEBRAND.

HELGA sits at her chamber door—
God only my heart from sorrow can sever!
She seweth the same seam o'er and o'er.
Let me tell of the sorrow that lives for ever!

What she should work with golden thread,
She works alway with silk instead;

What her fingers with silk should sew,
She works alway with the gold, I trow.

One whispereth in the ear of the Queen,
" Helga is sewing morning and e'en!

" Her seam is wildly and blindly done;
Down on the seam her tear-drops run!"

The good Queen hearkens wonderingly:
In at the chamber door goes she.

" Hearken unto me, little one !
    Why is thy seam so wildly done ? "

" My seam is wild and my work is mad,
    Because my heart is so sad—so sad !

" My father was a King so good—
    Fifty knights at his table stood.

" My father let me sew and spin.
    Twelve knights each strove my love to win :

" Eleven wooed me as lovers may,
    The twelfth he stole my heart away ;

" And he who wed me was Hildebrand,
    Son to a King of Engelland.

" Scarce did we our castle gain,
    When the news was to my father ta'en.

" My father summoned his followers then :
    ' Up, up ! and arm ye, my merry men !

" ' Don your breastplates and helmets bright,
    For Hildebrand is a fiend in fight ! '

" They knocked at the door with mailèd hand :
    ' Arise and hither, Sir Hildebrand ! '

" Sir Hildebrand kissed me tenderly :
    ' Name not my name, an' thou lovest me ;

" ' Even if I bleeding be,
    Name me never till life doth flee ! '

" Out at the door sprang Hildebrand,
    His good sword glistening in his hand,

" And ere the lips could mutter a prayer,
    Slew my five brothers with golden hair.

" Only the youngest slew not he—
    My youngest brother so dear to me.

" Then cried I loud, ' Sir Hildebrand,
    In the name of our Lady, stay thy hand !

" ' Oh, spare the youngest, that he may ride
    With the bitter news to my mother's side ! '

" Scarcely the words were utterèd,
    When Sir Hildebrand fell bleeding and dead.

" To his saddle my brother, fierce and cold,
    Tied me that night by my tresses of gold.

" Over valley and hill he speeds ;
    With thorns and brambles my body bleeds.

" Over valley and hill we fleet ;
    The sharp stones stick in my tender feet.

" Through deep fords the horse can swim ;
    He drags me choking after him.

" We came unto the castle great ;
    My mother stood weeping at the gate.

" My brother built a tower forlorn,
    And paved it over with flint and thorn ;

" My cruel brother placed me there,
  With only my silken sark to wear.

" Whene'er I moved in my tower forlorn,
  My feet were pierced with the sharp, sharp thorn.

" Whensoever I slept on the stones,
  Aches and pains were in all my bones.

" My brother would torture me twentyfold ;
  But my mother begged I might be sold.

" A clock was the price they took for me—
  It hangs on the Kirk of our Ladie.

" And when the clock on the kirk chimed first,
  The heart of my mother asunder burst."

  Ere Helga all her tale hath said,
(God only my heart from sorrow can sever !)
  On the arm of the Queen she is lying dead.
(Let me tell of the sorrow that lives for ever !)

THE WEE, WEE GNOME.

ON a hill that faced the western sea
    A peasant went to bide ;
He carried all his household there,
    And hawk and hound beside.
The wild deer, the wild, wild deer in the forest !

He carried with him hawk and hound,
    And built his house of wood ;
There were trees for stakes, and turfs for roof,
    And the wild, wild deer for food.

He felled the oak and the poplar white,
    And the silver beech also :
The sharp " clump ! clump ! " of his axe was heard
    By the gumlie gnomes below.

The gumlie gnomes in the hill that dwelt,
    Grumbled and gathered in crowd ;
They cried, while he felled his posts and staves,
    " Who is it knocks so loud ? "

Then up and spake the smallest gnome,—
  Small as a mouse was he,—
" It is a Christian man that knocks,
  I know it certainlie ! "

And up and spake the wee, wee gnome,
  So small, and spare, and thin :
" Let us unto the peasant's house,
  And hold our court within !

" He cutteth down our forest trees,
  Whose shade we love to see ;
But he shall as a guerdon give
  His own goodwife to me."

And all the gnomes that dwelt in the hill
  Joined hands in a wild delight,
Round and around they danced and danced
  To the door of the Christian wight.

Five score of gumlie gnomes they were,
  And seven beside, I weet,
And they will be the peasant's guests,
  And feast on his drink and meat.

The hound howled loudly at the gate,
    The herdsman his great horn blew,
The cattle lowed from stall to stall,
    And the gray and black cock crew.

The peasant from the window looked,
    And grew so pale with fear :
" Now help me, Jesus, Mary's Son !
    The gnomes are coming here !"

In every nook of every room
    He made the cross divine ;
And the gumlic gnomes in terror fled,
    For well they knew the sign.

And some fled east, and some fled west,
    And some fled north beside,
And some fled down to the deep, deep sea,
    And there they still abide.

But the wee, wee gnome, with glittering eyes,
    Lifted the great door-pin,
And trembled not at the cross's sign,
    But smiled and entered in.

The housewife forced a welcome smile,
   Curtsied, and spake him sweet ;
She sat him at the table board,
   And gave him oil and meat.

The wee, wee gnome he knit his brows,
   And slapt the table board :
Who gave thee leave to build thy house
   Where I am king and lord ?

" But if thou wilt beneath me dwell,—
   Mark what I say to thee,—
Ho ! thou must give thine own goodwife
   As guerdon and as fee."

Then answered back the trembling wight,
   And he was pale with fear,
" Sweet sir, take not mine own goodwife,
   Whom I esteem so dear !

" O gracious sir ! O gentle sir !
   You seem so sweet and kind ;
Take all my chattels and my gold,
   And leave my wife behind ! "

" Ho ! shall I take thy goods and gold
    To my cave as black as soot?
Ho ! shall I take thy wife and thee,
    And trample ye under foot ? "

The peasant and his household quake
    And eye each other in pain :
" Better, indeed, that one should go
    Than we should all be slain ! "

And up and stood the peasant then,
    And he was pale as foam,
He gave Eline his own goodwife
    Unto the wee, wee gnome.

The wee, wee gnome leapt up and laughed,
    And chucked her 'neath the chin !
Her knees grew weak, and her face grew pale,
    And her heart was cold within.

Her tears fell fast, as the wee, wee gnome
    Twinkled his glittering e'en :
" Now Heaven help a lost goodwife !
    —That I had never been !

"I married with as braw a man
    As may a-wooing go,
And shall I have this wee, wee gnome
    To be my bedfellow!"

He kissed her once, he kissed her twice,
    And wildly struggled she;
He was the ugliest wee, wee gnome
    That eye of man could see.

He kissed her once, he kissed her twice,
    She could not wrestle or run;
He kissed her twice, he kissed her thrice,
    She called on Mary's Son.

And when she called on Mary's Son,
    Oh, what a wondrous sight!
The ugly wee, wee gnome became
    A tall and comely knight.

"My stepmother put a curse on me,
    And made me a goblin gray,
But when you called on Mary's Son
    The curse was cast away.

" And since thou canst not," laughed the knight,
　" From thy dear husband go,
Oh, I will take thy daughter dear
　To be my bedfellow.

" But grace be thine, thou brave Eline,
　And be thy husband s too ;
May Mary's Son watch over thee,
　For thou art strong and true ! "

The peasant dwells on the hill by the sea,
　And the gnomes stay far, far down ;
His daughter in green England dwells,
　And wears a golden crown.

Now hath Eline, the true goodwife,
　Won honour to her home ;
She is mother to a bonnie Queen
　Who has wed the wee, wee gnome.

Now reigns the daughter of Eline,
　So queenly and fair of face ;
Eline bides still with her old goodman,
　And goes singing about the place,
The wild deer, the wild, wild deer in the forest.

THE TWO SISTERS.

ONE sister to the other spake,
    The summer comes, the summer goes!
"Wilt thou, my sister, a husband take?"
On the grave of my father the green grass grows!

"Man shall never marry me
    Till our father's death avengèd be."

"How may such revenge be planned?—
    We are maids, and have neither mail nor brand."

"Rich farmers dwell along the vale;
    They will lend us brands and shirts of mail."

They doff their garb from head to heel;
    Their white skins slip into skins of steel.

Slim and tall, with downcast eyes,
    They blush as they fasten swords to their thighs.

Their armour in the sunshine glares
As forth they ride on jet-black mares.

They ride unto the castle great :
Dame Erland stands at the castle gate.

" Hail, Dame Erland ! " the sisters say ;
" And is Herr Erland within to-day ? "

" Herr Erland is within indeed ;
With his guest he drinks the wine and mead."

Into the hall the sisters go ;
Their cheeks are paler than driven snow.

The maidens in the chamber stand :
Herr Erland rises with cup in hand.

Herr Erland slaps the cushions blue :
" Rest ye, and welcome, ye strangers two ! "

" We have ridden many a mile,
We are weary, and will rest awhile."

" Oh, tell me, have ye wives at home ?
Or are ye gallants that roving roam ? "

" Nor wives nor bairns have we at home,
  But we are gallants that roving roam."

" Then, by our Lady, ye shall try
  Two bonnie maidens that dwell hard by—

" Two maidens with neither mother nor sire,
  But with bosoms of down and eyes of fire."

  Paler, paler the maidens turn ;
  Their cheeks grow white, but their black eyes
      burn.

" If they indeed so beauteous be,
  Why have they not been ta'en by thee ? "

  Herr Erland shrugged his shoulders up,
  Laughed, and drank of a brimming cup.

" Now, by our Lady, they were won,
  Were it not for a deed already done :

  I sought their mother to lure away,
  And afterwards did their father slay ! "

Then up they leap, those maidens fair ;
Their swords are whistling in the air.

"This for tempting our mother dear ! "
Their red swords whirl, and he shrieks in fear.

"This for the death of our father brave !"
Their red swords smoke with the blood of the
knave.

They have hacked him into pieces, small
As the yellow leaves that in autumn fall.

Then stalk they forth, and forth they fare ;
They ride to a kirk, and kneel in prayer.

Fridays three they in penance pray,
The summer comes, the summer goes !
They are shriven, and cast their swords away.
On the grave of my father the green grass grows !

EBBE SKAMMELSON.

SIR SKAMMEL dwelt far north in Thy,
  And wealthy lands did own ;
Sir Skammel had five bonnie sons,
  And two were men full-grown.
Alone in the wild wood wanders Ebbe Skammelson !

The one was Ebbe Skammelson,
  The other Peter the young,
And sadder, darker fate than theirs
  Was never told nor sung.

Ebbe he saddled his charger gray,
  And galloped through greenwood glade,
And there with witching words he wooed
  The proud May Adelaide.

He wooed the proud May Adelaide,
  And like a lily was she ;
He bare her to his mother's house,
  And hied to a far countree.

But Ebbe stept to the high chamber
    Ere yet he hied away :
"While in the Court o' the King I serve,
    Think of me night and day.

"Think of me, Adelaide, my May,
    And of the love I give,
While in the Court o' the King I gain
    Red gold whereon to live."

And Ebbe in the Court o' the King
    Won gold and fame beside ;
At home Sir Peter, his young brother,
    Thought of the bonnie bride.

And Ebbe in the Court o' the King
    Gathered the red gold fast ;
Peter, his brother, built a ship,
    And cut a tree for mast.

Peter, his brother, built a boat,
    And launched it on the tide,
And sailed away to North Jutlànd,
    To Ebbe Skammelson's bride.

It was young Peter Skammelson
  Donned clothes of silk and fur,
And stept before sweet Adelaide
  All in the high chambèr.

" Hail unto thee, fair Adelaide !
  Come plight thy troth to me,
And all the days that I may live
  I 'll love and honour thee."

" How should I plight my troth to thee,
  How should I wed thee now,
When I to Ebbe Skammelson
  Have given my true-love vow ?

" I sware to wait for eight long years
  To all my kith and clan,—
The King himself forbade me eke
  To wed another man."

Then answered Peter Skammelson,
  " Ebbe roams far and free,
He serves in the Court o' the King, and makes
  Thy name a mockerie."

                                        c

Outspake young Peter's old mother
  A treasonous word, I wot,—
" Ay, marry Peter Skammelson,
  For Ebbe hath forgot.

" Ebbe serves in the Court o' the King,
  And doth thy true love wrong ;
A maid there is of the Queen's chamber
  Whom he hath courted long.

" Far better marry Peter, my son,
  With his red towers by the sea,
Than wait and pine for one who loves
  Another more than thee."

" Hearken, young Peter Skammelson,—
  Go seek another wife ;
I will not wed another man
  While Ebbe, thy brother, hath life."

It was Sir Peter's old mothèr
  Full cruellie she cried,
" Then hear the truth, May Adelaide,—
  Last hairst my Ebbe died ! "

Up stood the bonnie Adelaide,
  Slight as a lily wand ;
She gave to Peter Skammelson
  Her troth and white, white hand.

So gaily for the marriage feast
  They brewed the mead so clear ;
And Ebbe in the Court o' the King
  Did nought behold nor hear.

They brewed the wine and white, white mead,
  And two months passed away,
And then young Peter Skammelson
  Beheld his wedding-day.

It was young Ebbe Skammelson
  Woke up and cried in fright,
For he had dreamed a dreadful dream,
  All in the dead of night.

It was young Ebbe Skammelson
  Woke up at night and cried,
And spake about his dreadful dream
  To a comrade by his side.

" Methought that all my stone chamber
    Stood in a fiery glow,
And therein burst my young brother
    And Adelaide alsò."

" In sooth ? then, Ebbe Skammelson,
    Some scath is near at hand,
For when one dreams of flaming fire
    It bodes a naked brand.

" But if in dreams thy stone chamber
    All fiery seemed to be,
It bodeth Peter, thy young brothèr,
    Is wooing thy ladie."

It was Sir Ebbe Skammelson
    Fastened his sword to his side,
And, seeking out the King, gained leave
    To fatherland to ride.

It was Sir Ebbe Skammelson
    All eagerly homeward flew,
And what had been a seven days' ride
    Sir Ebbe rode in two.

It was Sir Ebbe Skammelson
    Rode swift upon his way,
And came unto his father's gate
    Upon the bridal day.

Up to his father's castle red
    Rode Ebbe Skammelson,
And at the porch stood a little page,
    And, whistling, leant thereon.

" Hearken, hearken, thou little page,
    And truly answer me :
Why is the place so blithe ? and why
    This merry companie ? "

" Here gather the ladies o' the North,
    Wha by the fjord abide,
And theirs are a' the chariots red
    Ye see on ilka side.

" Braw hae they decked thy brither's bride,
    And they are blithe and gay ;
The bonnie Lady Adelaide
    Thy brither weds the day ! "

Out came Ebbe's sisters twain,
    With golden cups in hand :
" Dear brother Ebbe Skammelson,
    Welcome to thy fatherland ! "

And it was Ebbe's sisters twain
    That kindly welcomed him ;
Father and mother welcomed him not ;
    The companie looked grim.

A bright gold bracelet unto each
    Gave Ebbe tenderlie,
And each gold bracelet he had earned
    To pleasure his ladie.

One sadly bade him tarry there,
    The other bade him go :
" If here thou tarriest to-night,
    'Twill surely bring us woe."

His father and mother asked him in
    To sit at the festal board ;
Pale went Ebbe Skammelson,
    And did not say a word.

He turned his horse around about,
　And sought to gallop away ;
His mother held the horse's rein,
　And begged Sir Ebbe to stay.

She led him to a cushioned stool,
　And bade him sit and dine ;
Then all the words that Ebbe said
　Were, "I will pour ye wine !"

He poured the wine for the bonnie bride,
　Clad all in pearls and gold,
And every time he looked at her
　His flesh and blood felt cold.

It was Sir Ebbe Skammelson
　Drank deep of the wine so red,
And last he craved his father's leave
　To hie away to bed.

Late in the quiet gloaming hour,
　When the dew began to fall.
The bonnie Lady Adelaide
　Walked from the banquet-hall.

They followed her unto her bower,
   Her bridal maidens fair,
And up came Ebbe Skammelson,
   And the bridal torch would bear.

It was Sir Ebbe Skammelson
   Paused on the balconie :
" Dost thou remember, Adelaide,
   The troth-plight sworn to me ? "

" All the love-troth I gave to thee,
   To Peter, thy brother, I give,
And I will be a mother to thee
   For all the days I live."

" I sought not thee my mother to be,
   I sought thee for my wife ;
Therefore shall Peter Skammelson
   Yield up his wicked life.

" Yet hearken, hearken, Adelaide,—
   Wilt take me by the hand ?
I will my traitor brother slay,
   And bear thee from the land."

" And if thou didst thy brother slay,
　　　How should that win my love ?
Nay ! I should grieve myself to death,
　　　As doth the turtle-dove."

It was Sir Ebbe Skammelson
　　　Spake not nor uttered sound,
Only he grew as white as snow,
　　　And stamped upon the ground.

He followed her unto her bower,
　　　And never a word he spoke ;
But Ebbe Skammelson he had
　　　A sword beneath his cloak.

In at the door Sir Ebbe stept,
　　　His drawn sword at his side,
And there beside the bridal bed
　　　He slew the bonnie bride !

With glittering sword he cut her down,
　　　While by her bed she stood ;
It was her bonnie crown of gold
　　　Lay swimming in her blood.

And underneath his cloak he hid
　　His sharp sword, dripping red.
And hied unto the banquet-hall,
　　And to the bridegroom said :

"Hearken, O Peter Skammelson,—
　　It is the midnight hour ;
Thy bonnie bride awaiteth thee
　　All in the bridal bower."

It was young Peter Skammelson
　　Went pale to hear and see ;
For all men saw that Ebbe's heart
　　Was wroth as wroth could be.

"Hearken, O Ebbe Skammelson,
　　All dearest brother mine !
I seek no more May Adelaide,
　　And freely make her thine.

"Hearken, O Ebbe Skammelson,
　　And lay thy wroth aside,—
I swear I hold the bridal nought,
　　And freely yield the bride."

" Stand up, thou Peter Skammelson,
 Hie to thy bridal bed ;
How bonnie look the bed and bower
 Bestrewn with roses red ! "

It was Sir Ebbe Skammelson
 Sprang over the banquet board,
And clove young Peter to the brain
 With his sharp and bloody sword.

Woe, woe, there was in hall and bower,
 And mickle terror and pain ;
Bridegroom and bride are lying dead,
 By fierce Sir Ebbe slain.

His father had a grievous wound,
 His mother lost a hand,
Therefore rides Ebbe Skammelson
 Exiled from fatherland.

His brother Peter Skammelson
 And Adelaide lay dead,
Wherefore, Sir Ebbe wanders wide,
 Begging his daily bread.

From such a bloody bridal day
   God shelter young and old :
The wine is bitter, the mead is sour
   Whenever the tale is told.
Alone in the wild wood wanders Ebbe Skammelson !

MAID METTELIL.

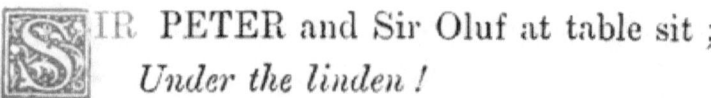

SIR PETER and Sir Oluf at table sit ;
  Under the linden !
They drink their red wine with words of wit.
Under the linden wakens my dearest !

" O hearken, Sir Oluf, boon comrade mine :
  Why pledge not thy troth to some maiden fine ? "

" And wherefore marry a housewife cold
  When I have my magical horn of gold ?

" Whenever upon my horn I play
  I can gain as many maids as I may ;

" Whenever upon my horn I play
  There is never a maiden can say me nay."

" I know a maiden in this countree
  Who never would answer ' ay ' to thee.

" I stake my horse—'tis a goodly steed—
  With Mette, my bride, thou canst never succeed."

" I stake my necklace of pearls of price,
  I 'd win her though she were made of ice."

II.

Late in the eve, in the gloaming shade,
Sir Oluf began to lure the maid.

Deftly he blew in his horn of gold :
Maid Mettelil heard him across the wold.

Long listens Maid Mettelil eagerly :
" Who playeth so sweetly to summon me ? "

Up and down swell her breasts of snow :
" Dare I thither by moonlight go ?

" If I thither by moonlight go,
  Never one of my maids must know."

III.

Maid Mettelil, and her hound so small,
Through the rose grove creep with light footfall.

Maid Mettelil, in a mantle blue,
Unto the bower of Sir Oluf flew.

She knocks at the door with her white, white
  hand—
"Open, Sir Oluf, for here I stand!"

"None have I summoned unto my bower;
None shall enter at gloaming hour."

"Open the door, Sir Oluf, to me—
Heart-sick am I with thy minstrelsie."

"Heart-sick art thou with my minstrelsie?
Nathless, you come not by night to me.

"Gladly would I welcome thee here,
Were not Sir Peter my comrade dear.

" And if I am grown so dear to thee,
   Still dearer thy husband is to me."

" Rise up, Sir Oluf, and open the door—
   On my forehead of white the damp dews pour."

" And fall the dews on thy forehead fair ?
   Hie thee homeward, and rest thee there."

" And if thou wilt not open the door,
   Let thy servant follow me, I implore."

" The moon is clear and the white stars burn—
   Alone thou hast come, and canst return.

" The moon shines clearly overhead,
   And will light thee safely to thy bed."

IV.

Maid Mettelil, and her hound so small,
   Are running homeward with light footfall.

To the castle gate they come full soon ;
   Sir Peter stands in the light of the moon.

" Welcome, Maid Mettelil, my bride !
   Where hast wandered at midnight tide ? "

" Out in the greenwood grove, I ween,
   Plucking the blossoms, the blue and the green :

" Plucking the blossoms, the red and white,
   That look so bonnie by pale moonlight.

" Yonder have I been wandering,
   Hearing the nightingale sweetly sing."

" No nightingale hast thou heard to-night,
   But only Sir Oluf's horn so bright.

" Hearken, O Mettelil, unto me :
   Thou hast made thy couch 'neath the linden tree.

" Now have I lost my steed, I ween,
   Since thou so shameless a bride hast been."

v.

And no man knew she had been so light,
But her bower was burnt to the ground that night.

D

It was my trusty huntsman
    Hung the owl on a forest tree,
To frighten away from my window
    All neighbours as hoarse as he.

But now the summer is over
    And the stork has winged away,
Gone are the many voices
    That rendered the greenwood gay

Among the leafless branches
    Low winds of the autumn creep,—
They weary me many a gloaming,
    And trouble my thoughts from sleep.

I think of the old owl often,
    When the nights are lonely and long
And I wish the owl were living,
    And let me list to his song.

THE ELF DANCE.

SIR OLUF, the knight, full wide hath rid,
    The guests to his wedding feast to bid.
But all in the moonlight the elves dance featly!

Lightly the elfin companie
Is dancing under the greenwood tree.

There dances four, there dances five—
How in their midst shall Sir Oluf thrive?

The Elf King's daughter is featest of all:
She grips his rein with her fingers small.

"Welcome, Herr Oluf! welcome to thee!
Hither, and tread in the dance with me."

"I dare not dance, and I must away,
For to-morrow is my bridal-day."

"Listen, Herr Oluf: dance with me—
Buck-skin boots will I give to thee!"

" I dare not dance, and I must away,
　For to-morrow is my bridal-day."

" Listen, Herr Oluf, listen to me—
　A silken sark I will give to thee !

" A silken sark, so white and fine,
　My mother wove it by pale moonshine."

" I dare not dance, and I must away,
　For to-morrow is my bridal-day."

" Listen, Herr Oluf : dance with me—
　A helmet of gold I will give to thee."

" A helmet of gold were fine to see ;
　But I dare not tread in the dance with thee."

" And wilt thou not tread in the dance with me ?
　Sickness and blight shall thy portion be !"

His shoulders she strikes with her fingers white :
Ne'er hath he felt a blow so light.

She lifts Sir Oluf upon his steed :
" Now off and away to thy lady speed ! "

Sir Oluf rides—he rides in fear :
At the gate is waiting his mother dear.

" Listen, Herr Oluf, my own bonnie knight :
Why are thy cheeks so ghastly white ? "

"Well may my cheeks be ghastly white,—
I have been in the Elf-wife's dance to-night."

" Listen, Herr Oluf, and woe betide !
What shall I say to thy dear young bride ? "

" Say I am gone to the wood hard by,
My horse and eke my hound to try."

Early at dawn, when it was day,
The bride came down in her bride-gear gay.

They drank of mead and they drank of wine :
" But where is Herr Oluf, bridegroom mine ? "

" Herr Oluf hath gone to the wood hard by,
   His horse and eke his hound to try."

She lifted up the curtains red—
   There lay Sir Oluf, and he was dead.

Early at dawn, when the sun was hie,
   From Sir Oluf's gate came corses three,—

Sir Oluf the knight, and his bonnie bride,
   And his broken-hearted mother beside.
But all in the moonlight the elves dance featly !

THE LOVER'S STRATAGEM.

IT was the young Herr Carl
    Fell sick, and sick he lay ;
He heard nor Mass nor even-song
    For many and many a day.
Thou waitest for me in the bower of roses, all-dearest !

Nor Mass nor even-song
    He heard for many a day ;
His sisters and his mother dear
    They nurse him as they may.

First step in his sisters,—
    They stand aloof in fear ;
But to his bed his mother creeps,
    And whispers in his ear :

" And say, my son, Herr Carl,
    Unto thy mother dear,
Is it a sickness of the flesh
    Wherein thou lingerest here ? "

" No sickness of the flesh
    Keepeth me lying here—
But 'tis the little maid, Eline,
    Whom I hold so dear, so dear ! "

" If little Maid Eline
    Maketh thy cheek so wan,
Rise up and ride unto her gate,
    And woo her like a man."

" Her father have I asked,
    And he hath answered me,
That I may never wed Eline
    Till I win her secretly."

Herr Carl arose in bed,
    So sad and sweet of mien ;
They have decked him in woman's gear,
    And called him Maid Christine.

It was the young Herr Carl,
    And forth to kirk went he ;
Bright golden gems are on his head.
    But his eyes droop bashfully.

Bright gems are on his head,
　　His robe is lily white,
But ye may hear how underneath
　　Jingles his armour bright !

Up peeps the fair Eline,
　　While all the people pray :
" And who is yonder stranger maid
　　That comes to kirk this day ? "

Answered the serving-maids—
　　And they were warned, I ween—
It is the sister of Herr Carl,
　　And she is called Christine."

It was the fair Eline,
　　A lily hand reached she :
' O will you hither, Maid Christine,
　　And keep me company ?

' O little Maid Christine,
　　Keep me companie ;
Full many a merry song and tale
　　I have to tell to thee.

" Many a merry tale
    Have I to tell to thee,
And how thy brother, young Herr Carl,
    Tried hard to wanton me."

It was the young Herr Carl
    Smiled in his sleeve, and said,
" Ne'er heard I that my brother Carl
    Had wantoned wife or maid."

But when the Mass was sung,
    And the priest had gone his way—
" I swear that thou shalt be my guest,
    O Maid Christine, to-day ! "

They ride across the fields,
    And through green groves they go,
And aye the hand of sweet Christine
    Holds the other's saddle-bow.

Then in the dusky eve
    The dews began to gloam ;
It was the little Maid Christine
    Rose up to journey home.

Then sware the fair Eline—
    By God and men sware she—
" The rude and drunken roam by night,
    And they might wanton thee ! "

Then sware the fair Eline—
    By God and man also—
" Here rest with me, sweet Maid Christine ;
    It is too late to go."

Into her sleeping-room
    Then went the fair Eline ;
And after, laughing in her sleeve,
    Tript little Maid Christine.

He doffed his robe of white,
    And eke his skirt of blue,
And, underneath, his suit of mail
    Glittered like golden dew.

Then marvelled fair Eline,
    Such glittering gear to mark :
" Oh, never saw I maid before
    Who wore so strange a sark ! "

" O tell me, fair Eline,
    And true as Heaven above,
Is there never man in all the world
    Whom thou couldst wed and love ?"

" No man in all the world,
    I swear by Heaven to thee,
Unless it be the young Herr Carl,
    Who ne'er may marry me !"

" And if thou lovest him—
    Herr Carl, dear brother mine—
I swear to thee, O fair Eline,
    He surely shall be thine !

" And if thou lovest him—
    Herr Carl, my brother dear—
Oh, turn and kiss him on the cheek,
    For he stand so near, so near !"

" O hearken, young Herr Carl,
    And kiss me not, I pray ;
My father gave my maiden life
    To the cloister yesterday ! "

Upon her throbbing heart
    His tender hand laid he :
" By the good craft that brought me here,
    Herewith I marry thee ! "

He kissed her on the cheek,
    He kissed her tenderlie :
" Oh, wilt thou now to cloister go,
    O fair Eline, from me ? "

And what care I for cloister ? "
    The little maiden laughed ;
" But let the bridal bells be rung,
    And the bridal cup be quaffed."

'Tis merry in the hall—
    Eline is fairly won—
They merrily drain the bridal cup,
    And are wed at rise o' sun,
Thou waitest for me in the bower of roses, all-dearest !

THE BONNIE GROOM.

"O SIT thee down, my bonnie groom,
  And play at dice with me."
" I have never a piece of red, red gold,
  Fair maid, to stake with thee."
The game is played, and hearts are lost and won !

" O stake thy hat, my bonnie groom,
  And either give or take :
My necklace of the white, white pearl
  Against thy hat I stake."

When first upon the table board
  The golden dice are played,
The bonnie groom hath lost his hat
  Unto the laughing maid.

" O sit thee down, my bonnie groom,
  And play at dice with me."
" I have never a piece of red, red gold,
  Fair maid, to stake with thee."

" O stake thy tunic, bonnie groom,
　　And either give or take :
Against thy tunic, poor and torn,
　　My crown of gold I stake."

When next upon the table board
　　The golden dice are played,
The groom hath lost his tunic poor
　　Unto the laughing maid.

" O sit thee down, my bonnie groom,
　　And play at dice with me."
" I have never a piece of red, red gold,
　　Fair maid, to stake with thee."

" O stake thy hose, my bonnie groom,
　　And add thy shoon beside :
I stake my honour and my troth,"
　　The laughing virgin cried.

When next upon the table board
　　The golden dice they pour,
The bonnie groom hath won the game,
　　And the maiden smiles no more.

"O hearken, hearken, bonnie groom ;
    I knew not what I said ;
My silver-handled knives of price
    I give to thee instead."

"Thy silver-handled knives of price
    At little worth I hold ;
But I will wed the maiden fair
    I have won with dice of gold."

"O hearken, hearken, bonnie groom ;
    I knew not what I said ;
And sarks and stockings, silken-sewn,
    I give to thee instead."

"Thy sarks and stockings, silken-sewn,
    At little worth I hold ;
But I will wed the maiden fair
    I have won with dice of gold."

"O hearken, hearken, bonnie groom ;
    I knew not what I said ;
A snow-white horse and saddle eke
    I give to thee instead."

" Thy snow-white horse and saddle eke
 At little worth I hold ;
But I will have the maiden fair
 I have won with dice of gold."

" O hearken, hearken, bonnie groom ;
 I knew not what I said ;
My castle and the wealth therein
 I give to thee instead."

" Thy castle and the wealth therein
 At little worth I hold ;
But I will wed the maiden fair
 I won with dice of gold."

The maiden rends her golden hair,
 And hides her pale, pale face :
" God help a wretched maiden, won
 By a wight so poor and base ! "

The bonnie groom stands up in court,
 And taps her with his sword :
" O I have won thee, maiden fair,
 And I am now thy lord !

"And yet am I no stable groom,
  Nor yet of low degree ;
 I am as bonnie and rich a prince
  As dwells in this countrie."

"Art thou a bonnie prince indeed,
  And not of low degree ?
 My love, my honour, and my troth
  I gladly give to thee."
The game is played, and hearts are lost and won !

CLOISTER ROBBING.

I'LL sing to ye a song,
  If ye will list to me,
Of how the young Sir Morten Dove
  Betrothed a fair ladye.
The roses and lilies grow bonnily !

Sir Morten loved fair Adelaide,
  And Adelaide loved him ;
But since the maid had little gear,
  His friends looked black and grim.

So full of wrath were one and all,
  When the strange news was spread :
They prayed the Lord who rules the world,
  The two might never wed.

Sir Morten's father drove him forth
  Into a strange countrie,
And Adelaide was to cloister borne,
  Though sorely struggled she.

And young Herr Morten dwelt afar
    For weary winters nine,
And all the while for his true-love
    Did nought but fret and pine.

So sore the young Sir Morten yearned
    To see his winsome May,
Though it should be his death, he would
    No longer stay away.

It was the young Sir Morten hied
    Home to his own countrie ;
But there they carried unto him
    Tidings of miserie.

Ah ! bitter, bitter was the tale
    They whispered in his ear,—
That they had to the cloister borne
    The maid he held so dear.

Unto his father dear he spake.
    " O father, father, hark !
My foes have given my own true-love
    Unto the cloister dark ! "

" O dry thine eyes, my son, my son,
    And hearken unto me :
The maid that waits to be thy bride
    Is twice as rich as she.

" Unto a bonnier, richer May
    Thou soon shalt give thy hand ;
Little red gold hath Adelaide,
    And less of rich green land."

" Sweeter to me my own true-love,
    With nought but her red dress,
Than the rich daughter of Sir Stig,
    And all she will possess !

" And what care I for rich green land ?
    And what care I for wealth ?
I care but for my own true-love,
    Whom I have won in stealth.

" And what care I for kinsmen,
    Were they thrice as high in worth ?
Yea, I will seek my own true-love,
    Though ye hound me o'er the earth."

Then whispered with his brother dear
    The young Sir Morten Dove :
" And how may I from cloister steal
    Away my own true-love ? "

" Go, deck thyself in grave-clothes white,
    And lay thee in a shell,
And I will to the cloister ride,
    The bitter tale to tell."

He decked himself in grave-clothes white,
    And lay in death-shell cold ;
Herr Nilans to the cloister rode
    And the bitter tale was told.

" Hail unto ye, O holy maids,
    And great shall be your gain,
if my dear brother Morten's corse
    May in your walls be lain."

All silent sat the holy maids,
    In black, black raiment all—-
Only the sweet maid Adelaide
    Let work and scissors fall.

Then cried the sweet maid Adelaide,
    With tears upon her face,
" Yea ! bury Morten, if ye list,
    Here in this holy place.

" Yea, here, in holy cloister-kirk,
    Bury his sweet young clay,
And daily where he lies asleep
    I 'll kneel me down and pray !

" I was a little child when first
    I heard him sue and woo ;
The Powers of heaven know full well
    That I have loved him true.

" His cruel father drove him off
    Into a strange countrie,
And into these dark cloister walls
    Against my will brought me."

It was Sir Nilans bent his head,
    And whispered in her ear,
" Ah, dry thine eyes, Maid Adelaide,
    And be of happy cheer."

" Never shall I forget my woe !
    Never forget my wrong !
For murdered is my own true-love,
    Whom I have loved so long."

Sorely she wept, Maid Adelaide,
    And her wet eyes were red,
When through the dismal cloister gate
    They brought Sir Morten, dead.

She crept unto Sir Morten's bier,
    And prayed to Heaven above :
" I loved thee, Morten, to the end,
    As never maid did love ! "

She lighted up the wax lights two,
    And sat her by his side :
" I would to God, dear love, that I
    Had in my cradle died.

" Nine winters, while thou wert away,
    Here weary life I led,
And never saw thy face again
    Until I saw thee dead ! "

And bitterly wept Adelaide,
   Wringing her hands so white.
Herr Morten heard her in his shell,
   Laughed loud, and rose upright.

Oh, up he stood, and gazed again
   On her he loved the best,
And tossed the gloomy grave-clothes off.
   And caught her to his breast.

" O hearken, hearken, my own true-love,
   Put all thy grief aside ;
Thou shalt from cloister follow me.
   And be my bonnie bride !

" Black are the horses that await
   In the kirkyard there without,
And black in suits of iron mail
   Await my henchmen stout."

Softly Sir Morten led her forth
   Out of the chapel wall,
And over her shoulders, for a cloak.
   He threw the sable pall.

All silent stood the cloister maids,
    Reading by candle-light;
They thought it was an angel bore
    Their sister off by night.

All silent stood the holy maids,
    Save only two or three.
" That such an angel," murmured these,
    " Would come by night for me ! "

Honour to young Sir Morten Dove !
    His heart was staunch and stout.
He bore her to his dwelling-house,
    And bade the bells ring out.

Honour to young Sir Morten Dove,
    And to his sweet ladye !
May more such maids be carried off
    By angels such as he !
The roses and lilies grow bonnily !

AGNES.

I.

MAID AGNES musing sat alone
    Upon the lonely strand;
The breaking waves sighed oft and low
    Upon the white sea-sand.

Watching the thin white foam, that broke
    Upon the wave, sat she.
When up a beauteous merman rose
    From the bottom of the sea.

And he was clad unto the waist
    With scales like silver white,
And on his breast the setting sun
    Put rosy gleams of light.

The merman's spear a boat-mast was,
    With crook of coral brown,
His shield was made of turtle-shell,
    Of mussel-shells his crown.

His hair upon his shoulders fell,
   Of bright and glittering tang;
And sweeter than the nightingale's
   Sounded the song he sang.

" And tell to me, sweet merman,
   Fresh from the deep, deep sea,
When will a tender husband come
   To woo and marry me?"

" O hearken, sweetest Agnes,
   To the words I say to thee—
All for the sake of my true heart,
   Let me thy husband be.

" Far underneath the deep, deep sea,
   I reign in palace halls,
And all around, of crystal clear,
   Uprise the wondrous walls.

" And seven hundred handmaids wait,
   To serve my slightest wish—
Above the waist like milk-white maids,
   Below the waist, like fish.

" Like mother-of-pearl the sea-sledge gleams,
   Wherein I journey crowned,
Along the sweet green path it goes,
   Dragged by the great seal-hound.

" And all along the green, green deeps
   Grow flowers wondrous fair ;
They drink the wave, and grow as tall
   As those that breathe the air."

Fair Agnes smiled, and stretched her arms,
   And leapt into the sea,
And down beneath the tall sea-plants
   He led her tenderlie.

II.

Eight happy years fair Agnes dwelt
   Under the green-sea wave,
And seven beauteous little ones
   She to the merman gave.

She sat beneath the tall sea-plants,
   Upon a throne of shells,
And from the far-off land she heard
   The sound of sweet kirk bells.

Unto her gentle lord she stept,
    And softly took his hand :
"And may I once, and only once,
    Go say my prayers on land?"

"Then hearken, sweet wife Agnes,
    To the words I say to thee—
Fail not in twenty hours and four
    To hasten home to me."

A thousand times "Good night" she said
    Unto her children small,
And ere she went away she stooped,
    And softly kissed them all ;

And, old and young, the children wept
    As Agnes went away,
And loud as any cried the babe
    Who in the cradle lay.

Now Agnes sees the sun again,
    And steps upon the strand—
She trembles at the light, and hides
    Her eyes with her white hand.

Among the folk she used to know,
     As they walk to kirk, steps she,
" We know thee not, thou woman wild,
     Come from a far countrie."

The kirk bells chime, and into kirk
     And up the aisle she flies ;
The images upon the walls
     Are turning away their eyes !

The silver chalice to her lips
     She lifteth tremblinglie,
For that her lips were all athirst.
     Under the deep, deep sea.

She tried to pray, and could not pray.
     And still the kirk bells sound ;
She spills the cup of holy wine
     Upon the cold, cold ground.

When smoke and mist rose from the sea,
     And it was dark on land,
She drew her robe about her face,
     And stood upon the strand.

F

Then folded she her thin, thin hands,
　　The merman's weary wife :
" Heaven help me in my wickedness,
　　And take away my life !"

She sank among the meadow grass,
　　As white and cold as snow ;
The roses growing round about
　　Turned white and cold alsò.

The small birds sang upon the bough,
　　And their song was sad and deep—
" Now, Agnes, it is gloaming hour,
　　And thou art going to sleep."

All in the twilight, when the sun
　　Sank down behind the main,
Her hands were pressed upon her heart,
　　And her heart had broke in twain.

The waves creep up across the strand,
　　Sighing so mournfullie,
And tenderly they wash the corse
　　To the bottom of the sea.

Three days she stayed beneath the sea,
 And then came back again,
And mournfully, so mournfully,
 Upon the sand was lain.

And, sweetly decked by tender hands,
 She lay a-sleeping there,
And all her form is wreathed with weeds,
 And a flower was in her hair.

The little herd-boy drove his geese
 Seaward at peep o' day,
And there, her hands upon her breast,
 Sweet Agnes sleeping lay.

He dug a grave behind a stone,
 All in the soft sea-sand,
And there the maiden's bones are dry,
 Though the waves creep up the strand.

Each morning and each evening,
 The stone is wet above ;
The merman hath wept (the town girls say)
 Over his lost true-love.

HOW SIR TONNE WON HIS BRIDE.

SIR TONNE forth from Alsö fares,
　　With his good sword by his side,
Whether it be on sea or land,
　A hero trusty and tried.
　　　　　　　Listen to my rune!

Herr Tonne in the rose grove rides,
　He rides to hunt the hare,
And there he spies the dwarf's daughter
　Among her maidens fair.

Herr Tonne in the rose grove rides,
　To hunt the hind rides he,
And there he spies the dwarf's daughter
　Under the linden tree.

With golden harp in hand, she lies
    Under a linden fair :
" See, yonder where Sir Tonne rides,
    And hunts the hind and hare.

' Sit down, sit down, my maidens small,
    And my little foot-page alsò,
While I play a rune, and cause the flowers
    O'er field and mead to grow."

Upon her harp of gold she struck,
    And played a Runic lay :
The wild, wild fowl forgot his song
    And listened on the spray.

The wild, wild fowl upon the spray
    Forgot to pipe and sing ;
The wild, wild hart on greenwood path
    Paused in the act to spring.

The meadow flowered, the greenwood bloomed,
    So wondrous was the song ;
Deep, deep Sir Tonne spurred his steed,
    But could not move along.

The meadow flowered, the greenwood bloomed—
   Sir Tonne could not ride;
Lightly he sprang from off his horse,
   And sat him by her side.

" Hail unto thee, O dwarf's daughter !
   And wilt thou be my May ?
And I will love and honour thee
   Until my dying day.

" Hail unto thee, O dwarf's daughter !
   A rose among lilies thou art !
There is never a man who longs so much
   To wear thee in his heart."

" Hearken, Sir Tonne, hearken,
   Talk not of love to me !
I have a lover, and the King
   Of all the Dwarfs is he.

" My father sits in the mountain,
   Among his men sits he ;
And in a month I shall be wed,
   With feast and melodie !

" My mother sits in the mountain,
 Spinning with golden thread ;
But I have crept away from her
 To strike the gold harp red."

" Ere the Dwarf King shall marry thee,
 Foul, foul shall be his fall ;
Ho ! I will lose my life, or break
 My sword in pieces small."

Answered the weird dwarf's daughter,
 And softly answered she :
" A fairer maid shall be thy May,
 Thou ne'er canst marry me !

" Haste, haste away, Herr Tonne !
 As fast as thou canst ride ;
My father and my lover fierce
 Will soon be at my side."

It was her dear, dear mother,
 Out of the hill peered she,
And there she saw Herr Tonne stand
 Under the linden tree.

Out came her dear, dear mother,
 And she was wroth, I ween.
" Now, wherefore, Alfhild, daughter mine,
 Sit here in the forest green ?

" Better, better thy linen sew
 Within the mountain old,
Than here within the rose grove sit
 And strike thy harp of gold.

" The King of Dwarfs hath feasted thee
 All for thy honeymoon—
Shame, shame ! to meet Sir Tonne here,
 And bind him with a rune."

It was the weird dwarf's daughter,
 Unto the cave hied she,
And young Sir Tonne followed her,
 But could not hear nor see.

Upon a stool, within the cave,
 The dwarf's wife spread a cloak,
And there Sir Tonne sat in trance,
 But at cock-crow he awoke.

The dwarf's wife opened her mystic book,
　　All in the cavern dim,
And freed Sir Tonne from the spell
　　Her daughter had cast on him.

" Now have I freed thee from the rune,
　　And cast the spell away ;
And this I did for honour's sake,
　　And thou art safe for aye.

" And I for love and right goodwill,
　　A goodlier gift will give ;
And I will woo a maid for thee,
　　Fairest of all that live.

" For I was reared of Christian folk,
　　And stolen here to wean :
I have a sister dear to me,
　　And named the Queen Christine.

" She bears a crown in Iceland,
　　And a Queen's proud name also :
Her daughter once was stolen away
　　Many a year ago.

" Her daughter once was stolen away,
     And the search was long and drear,
   And never now at kirk or dance
     They see that daughter dear.

" She dares not from her window peep,
     They watch her so in fear;
   She dare not play at chess with the King,
     Unless the Queen be near.

" Save that old King, her gentle eyes
     Have seen no mortal wight;
   Her mother locks with lock and bolt
     Her chamber door at night.

" This maiden sits in Upsal,
     And they name her Ermelin,
   And steel, and bolt, and iron ring
     From lovers lock her in.

" The old King's brother hath a son,
     Who is the old King's heir—
   Sir Allerod will have the throne,
     And wed the maiden fair.

" And I will give thee saddle and horse,
    And spurs of gold beside ;
How wild soe'er thy path may be,
    Thou shalt in safety ride.

" And I will give thee clothes of price,
    With golden seams and hems ;
And I will give thee the red shield, deckt
    With precious stones and gems ;

" And I will give thee a golden scroll,
    Where runes are wrought by me ;
And every word thou utterest
    Like written speech shall be."

Out spake Alfhild, the dwarf's daughter,
    For well she loved the knight :
" And I will give a trusty sword,
    And a lance all burnished bright ;

" And thou shalt never miss the way,
    However wild it be ;
And thou shalt never fight with foe,
    But gain the victorie ;

" And thou shalt safely come to land
    Whene'er thou sailest the sea ;
And never by a man on earth
    Shall thy body wounded be."

It was the dwarf's wife, Thorelil,
    Filled out the wine so clear :
" Haste, haste upon thy way, before
    My husband cometh near."

Herr Tonne in the rose grove rode,
    With glittering lance rode he,
And there he met the dwarf himself
    A-riding moodily.

" Well met, well met, Sir Tonne ;
    But wherefore thus away ?
And whither doth thy charger step
    So gallantly, I pray ? "

" I ride unto a distant place,
    To pluck a bonnie rose ;
And I am bold to break a lance
    With the doughtiest of foes."

" Ride on, ride on, and fare thee well—
    Ride on, my gallant knight—
At Upsal waits a champion stout,
    And all athirst for fight."

Herr Tonne swiftly rode along
    Till he came to Swedish ground,
And there beneath the greenwood boughs
    Ten arméd knights he found.

On every head a helmet bright,
    A shield on every breast,
At every side a glittering sword,
    And a shining lance in rest.

" Hail unto ye, O Swedish knights,
    That gather arméd here,
And will ye fight for gold, or fame.
    Or for your true-loves dear ? "

Answered the slim Prince Allerod,
    Proud to the red heart's core,
" Ho ! I have honour and red, red gold.
    And seek to win no more ;

" But there in Upsal dwells a maid,
　　By name Maid Ermelin,
And he who conquers in the joust
　　Shall that sweet lady win."

The first joust they together rode,
　　With wondering knights around,
Their shields were shattered, and their spears
　　Drove deep into the ground.

The second joust the warriors rode,
　　They met at topmost speed,
And Allerod with broken neck
　　Was hurled from off his steed.

Then fiercely strove those Swedish knights
　　To venge their leader's fall ;
But young Sir Tonne waved his sword,
　　And overthrew them all.

And up they picked their mantles blue,
　　Moodily muttering,
And off they rode into the west,
　　And stood before the King.

" A Jutish knight hath come to land,
  With neither fame nor name ;
Eight warriors hath he overthrown,
  And made them blush for shame.

" Eight warriors hath he overthrown,
  And put them all to flight,
And he hath slain thy brother's son,
  Young Allerod the knight."

Then answered back the fierce old King,
  With long and silver hair,
" Revenge me on that traitor knight.
  And ye shall sable wear."

Out rode those angry Swedish knights,
  The precious prize to gain ;
But in a trice those Swedish knights
  Were overthrown again ;

And skin of calf they still must wear,
  Not sable rich and gay ;
Yea ! skin of calf they still must wear
  And cloth of wadmel gray.

It was the angry Swedish knights
 Turned wild and shamed and wan :
There lives no man in all the world
 Could beat this Jutland man.

Herr Tonne still in Upsal rides
 With glittering sword and spear ;
His foemen thank the Lord they live,
 And sneak away in fear.

He slew the bear that watched the door.
 And broke the great door-pin,
And gazed upon the captive maid,
 The sweet Maid Ermelin.

The Swedish courtiers silent were,—
 They dared not speak a word,
For of this gallant Jutland knight
 Such wonders they had heard.

He hurled aside the Swedish knights,
 And slew the lion and bear,
And entered in the high chamber,
 And freed the maiden fair.

And there was joy in Iceland,
  When the tidings there were ta'en,
Joy in the hearts of King and Queen,
  That their child was found again.

Herr Tonne now in Iceland
  The old King's crown doth wear,
And blooming sweetly by his side
  Sits Ermelin the Fair.
                    Listen to my rune !

SIR MORTEN OF FOGELSONG.

IT was Sir Morten of Fogelsong,
   He rode in greenwood lawn,
And there a fatal blow gat he,
   All in the morning dawn.
Dead rides Sir Morten of Fogelsong !

To kirk he gave the red, red gold,
   To cloister gave his horse ;
All in the black and chilly earth
   They laid Sir Morten's corse.

It was the young Sir Folmer Skot—
   He swiftly galloped along—
For, craving speech, behind him rode
   Sir Morten of Fogelsong.

" O hearken, young Sir Folmer Skot,
    Rein in and talk with me,
For by my faith in Christ the Lord,
    I will not injure thee ! "

" O hearken, dark Sir Morten ;
    How ridest thou here to-day ?
They tolled the church bells yesternight,
    And laid thy corse in clay ! "

" I ride not here to sue for gifts,
    Nor doomed to ride for wrong,
But only for a plot of ground
    Forsworn to Fogelsong.

" I ride not here for red, red gold,
    And unto thee make moan ;
I ride here for the plot of ground
    Two fatherless bairns should own.

" O haste to Mettelil, my wife,
    And tell her my behest :
Until she yield the ground again,
    My soul can never rest !

" And if fair Mettelil, my wife,
 Should doubt thee or deny,
Say that without my chamber door
 My chamber slippers lie.

" Say that my chamber slippers lie
 Without my chamber door,
And if she look at dead of night,
 They will be full of gore."

" Ride back, ride back, Sir Morten,
 And slumber peacefullie ;
The fatherless bairns shall have their own,
 By Christ I swear to thee ! "

Black was Sir Morten's horse,
 Black was Sir Morten's hound,
And black, black were the ghostly folk
 That followed him into the ground.

But grace to fair Dame Mettelil !
 She heard her lord's behest :
The fatherless held their own again,
 And Sir Morten's soul had rest.
Dead rides Sir Morten of Fogelsong !

THE LEAD-MELTING.

'TWAS clear, cold, starry, silver night,
  And the old year was a-dying,
Three pretty girls with melted lead
  Sat gaily fortune-trying.
They dropt the lead in water clear,
  With blushing palpitations,
And as it hissed, with fearful hearts
  They sought its revelations.

In the deep night, while all around
  The snow was whitely falling,
Each pretty girl looked down to find
  Her future husband's calling :
The eldest sees a castle grand
  Girt round by shrubland shady,
And, blushing bright, she feels in thought
  A lady rich already !

The second sees a silver ship,
    And bright and glad her face is :
Oh, she will have a skipper bold,
    Grown rich in foreign places !
The youngest sees a glittering crown,
    And starts in consternation,
For Molly is too meek to dream
    Of reaching regal station.

And time went by,—one maiden got
    Her landsman, one her sailor—
The lackey of a country count !
    The skipper of a whaler !
And Molly has her crown, although
    She unto few can show it—
Her crown is true-love, fancy-wrought,
    Her husband,—a poor Poet !

YOUNG AXELVOLD.

THE King's men ride in merry greenwood.
　　To hunt the hart and hind,
And lying under a linden tree
　　A little child they find.
In the greenwood slumbers fair Ellen!

They lifted up the bonnie boy,
　　They wrapt him in mantle blue,
They bore him back to the King's own Court.
　　And found him a nurse so true.

They carried him forth when all was still.
　　To christen him by night;
They christened him young Axelvold,
　　All in the pale moonlight.

They fostered him in winters cold,
　　In winters cold full three ;
He blossomed to the sweetest flower
　　The eye of man could see.

They fostered him for fifteen years,
　　In sun and snow and wind ;
He grew to be the bravest youth
　　That hunted hart and hind.

The King's men shoot upon the lawn,
　　With jest and loud acclaim :
Who shoots like young Herr Axelvold
　　He puts them all to shame.

The King's men gather on the lawn,
　　And shoot with arrow and bow ;
They gnaw the trembling under lip
　　That he should shame them so.

" Far better run unto thy nurse,
　　And ask thy mother's name,
Than meet the honourably born,
　　And put them all to shame."

Then answered back young Axelvold,
    His cheeks were white with pain :
" I 'll know the name of my mother dear
    Before we meet again !"

It is the fair young Axelvold,
    His bonnie brow he knits,
He strideth to the high chamber
    Where his foster-mother sits.

" God save thee, foster-mother dear !
    And listen unto me :
Tell me the name of my dear mother,
    For it is known to thee."

" God save thee, dearest Axelvold !
    And listen unto me :
I know not the name of thy dear mother,
    Whether living or dead she be."

It was the pale young Axelvold,
    He drew his glittering knife :
" Name me the name of my dear mother,
    Or yield me up thy life !"

" Then sheathe thy knife, and hasten down,
    And heed what thou art told—
Thy mother in the palace sits,
    And wears a crown of gold."

It is the fair young Axelvold,
    To the women's hall hies he,
Among the matrons and the maids
    That sit in company.

And some are brown, and some are fair,
    And some white-haired and old,
And Ellen is the fairest there,
    And wears the crown of gold.

" God save ye, wives and maidens eke,
    Maidens and matrons dear !
God also save my sweet mother,
    If she be sitting here."

And silent sat the women all,
    And none dared breathe a breath ;
But Ellen plucked her crown away,
    And grew as pale as death.

" God save thee, then, my true mother,
    That wear'st the crown of gold !
Where is the son you left asleep
    All in the greenwood cold ?"

Fair Ellen stood with downcast eyes.
    And heart that wildly stirred ;
Her cheeks grew pale as the ash of fire.
    And she answered not a word.

She took the gold brooch from her breast.
    The crown from off her brow :
" Ne'er left I son in greenwood cold,
    By God and our Lady I vow !"

" O hearken to me, dear mother mine !
    And blushest thou not for shame,
That thou from such a son so long
    Hast hid thy name and fame ?

" O hearken, dearest mother mine !
    By the tears ye cause to me,
Name me the name of him who put
    The shame on thy son and thee !"

Fair Ellen clutched her brooch of gold,
   And eke her golden crown,
She held her hand upon her heart,
   With moist eyes drooping down.

" Haste, haste thee to the palace hall,
   Where they drink red wine and white ;
Thy father at the table sits
   With many a goodly knight.

" Haste, haste thee to the palace hall,
   Where they drink both mead and wine :
For there the king's son Erland sits,
   With a calm proud smile like thine !"

It is the fair young Axelvold,
   His cheeks are brightening ;
He strides into the banquet-hall
   Before the Danish King.

" All hail, ye knights and merry men,
   Who drink the wine and mead !
All hail, my dearest father too,
   If thou be here indeed !

" All hail, O dearest father mine !
    And blushest thou not for shame ?
A foundling thing they call the son
    Who is meet to bear thy name !"

All frowning sit the king's men all,
    And never a word they speak ;
Only the King's son Erland stirs,
    With a blush upon his cheek.

Only the King's son Erland speaks,
    And him all eyes behold :
" I am not thy father, by my troth
    I swear it, Axelvold !"

It was the pale young Axelvold,
    He drew his glittering knife :
" Thou shalt wipe my mother's shame away,
    Or yield me up thy life !

" O shame ! among these goodly knights
    To be so basely styled !
Shame to be named as basely born,
    Yet be a prince's child !"

Up sprang Prince Erland eagerly, ·
    And a smile was on his face :
" Thou worthy art to be called my son,
    I swear, by Heaven's grace !

" Thou art indeed, young Axelvold,
    As brave a knight as stands,
And Ellen is my own true wife,
    And thou shalt join our hands !"

'Tis merry, 'tis merry, in palace hall,
    Morning and eventide ;
Young Axelvold gives his mother away,
    And she is a prince's bride !

It was the brave young Axelvold
    Was blithe as ever a one :
" Last night I was a foundling base,
    To-day am a prince's son !"
In the greenwood slumbers fair Ellen !

THE JOINER.

"WHY planest thou with weary moan,
    Pale youth, by midnight and alone?
Why is thy cheek so thin and ghast?
Why do thy still tears fall so fast?"

" The work I do must all be done
    Ere the red rising of the sun;
Wherefore at dead of night I plane,
So thin and ghast, with mickle pain!"

" Why must thou work while others sleep?
    While others smile, why must thou weep?
Though here thou moanest, planing slow,
Of old thou wert a gay fellow."

" My hope, my joy, have wholly died—
    My girl became another's bride;
God also held her very dear,
For, see! I make her coffin here."

AAGE AND ELSIE.

IT was the young Herr Aage,
    He rode in summer shade,
To pay his troth to Elsie,
    The rosy little maid.

He paid his troth to Elsie,
    And sealed it with red, red gold ;
But ere a month had come and gone
    He lay in kirkyard mould.

It was the little Elsie,
    Her heart was clayey cold,
And young Herr Aage heard her moan
    Where he lay in kirkyard mould.

Uprose the young Herr Aage,
    Took coffin on his back,
And walked by night to Elsie's bower,
    All through the forest black.

Then knocked he with his coffin,
    He knocked and tirled the pin :
" Rise up, my bonnie Elsie lil,
    And let thy lover in !"

Then answered little Elsie,
    " I open not the door
Unless thou namest Mary's Son,
    As thou couldst do before."

" Stand up, my little Elsie,
    And open thy chamber door,
For I have named sweet Mary's Son,
    As I could do before."

It is the little Elsie,
    So worn, and pale, and thin,
She openeth the chamber door
    And lets the dead man in.

H

His dew-damp dripping ringlets
  She kaims with kaim of gold,
And aye for every lock she curls
  Lets fall a tear-drop cold.

" O listen, dear young Aage !
  Listen, all dearest mine !
How fares it with thee underground
  In that dark grave of thine ?"

" Whenever thou art smiling,
  When thy bosom gladly glows,
My grave in yonder dark kirkyard
  Is hung with leaves of rose ;

" Whenever thou art weeping,
  And thy bosom aches full sore,
My grave in yonder dark kirkyard
  Is filled with living gore.

" Hark ! the red cock is crowing,
  And the dawn gleams chill and gray,
The dead are summoned back to the grave,
  And I must haste away,

" Hark ! the black cock is crowing,
    'Twill soon be break of day—
The gate of heaven is opening,
    And I must haste away ! "

Up stood the pale Herr Aage,
    His coffin on his back,
Wearily to the cold kirkyard
    He walked through the forest black.

It was the little Elsie,
    Her beads she sadly told—
She followed him through the forest black,
    Unto the kirkyard cold.

When they had passed the forest,
    And gained the kirkyard cold,
The dead Herr Aage's golden locks
    Were gray and damp with mould ;

When they had passed the kirkyard,
    And the kirk had entered in,
The young Herr Aage's rosy cheeks
    Were ghastly pale and thin.

" O listen, little Elsie,
　　All-dearest, list to me !
　O weep not for me any more,
　　For I slumber tranquillie.

" Look up, my little Elsie,
　　Unto the lift so gray,
　Look up unto the little stars,—
　　The night is winging away."

She raised her eyes to heaven,
　　And the stars that glimmered o'er,
　Down sank the dead man to his grave—
　　She saw him never more.

Home went little Elsie,
　　Her heart was chilly cold,
　And ere a month had come and gone
　　She lay in kirkyard mould.

AXEL AND WALBORG;

OR,

THE COUSINS.

I. SIR AXEL BETROTHS THE CHILD WALBORG.

THEY scattered dice on the golden board,
    And blithe and merry were they;
The two fair ladies face to face,
    Smiled at the wondrous play.
The wheel of Fortune goes round and round.

And up and down were scattered the dice,
    And round and round they rolled;
And round goes Fortune's wheel, too swift
    For mortals to behold.

Dame Juliet and Queen Malfred
    The white dice nimbly threw;
And on the floor, with apples and pears,
    The bairn was playing too.

The bonnie bairn with apples and flowers
　　Was playing on the ground,
When in Sir Axel Thorsen stept,
　　And he for Rome was bound.

He greeted the dames and maidens fair,
　　For a courteous knight was he ;
He smiled upon the bonnie bairn,
　　And took her on his knee.

He tapped her on the white, white cheek,
　　For dear to him was she :
" Now, would thou wert a woman grown,
　　Mine own true-love to be ! "

Then, covered o'er with seams of gold,
　　His youngest sister said,
" Were she a woman grown this night,
　　Ye twain could never wed ! "

Then up and spake his mother dear,
　　And true, I ween, spake she :
" My son, ye are too near of kin,
　　Though equal in degree."

For plaything to the bonnie bairn
   He gave his golden ring :
The gift, ere she was woman grown,
   Had set her sorrowing.

" Now, mark thou well, my little bride,
   We twain betrothen are ;
And now I leave thy side, to fight
   For foreign kings afar."

II. SIR AXEL'S RETURN FROM AFAR.

'Tis bright, bright where Sir Axel rides,
   As out of the land he hies ;
'Tis dark, dark in the cloister walls
   Where his little true-love lies.
The wheel of Fortune goes round and round.

In cloister walls she learns to read,
   And silken seams she sews ;
She turns into a maiden fair,
   The bonniest flower that grows.

She turns into a maiden fair,
  And maidenly things is taught ;
And strange old songs and ancient lore
  Sweeten her face with thought.

Eleven years she in cloister dwelt,
  Until her mother died,
And she was ta'en to the Queen's own Court,
  And set at the Queen's own side.

Sir Axel serves in the Emperor's Court,
  With golden spurs at heel,
And many are the knightly deeds
  Done by his glittering steel.

Sir Axel, sweetly stretched in sleep,
  Full fair and still doth seem ;
But in the dead of night he groans,
  And hath a fearful dream.

Sir Axel in the high chamber
  On silken cushions lies,
But dreams he sees his own true-love
  Stand pale before his eyes ;

He dreams he sees sweet Walborg stand
    Clad in her velvet dress,
And at her side Prince Hogen stoops,
    Wooing in tenderness.

Early at morning, at dawn o' day,
    When the laverock singing rose,
Up leapt Sir Axel from his bed,
    And tremblingly donn'd his clothes.

Swiftly he saddled his good gray steed,
    Swiftly he galloped along ;
Sadly he sought to forget his dream,
    And hark to the wood-bird's song.

It was Sir Axel Thorsen,
    Through the rose grove bent his way,
And there, all in the morning-time,
    He met a pilgrim gray.

" Well met ! Good day, thou pilgrim gray !
    What may thy errand be ?
Now, from thy raiment it is clear
    Thou art from my countrie ! "

" Norway it is my fatherland ;
    From Gildish race I come ;
And, bent to look upon the Pope,
    I drag my way to Rome."

" If thou art sprung of Gildish race,
    Then near of kin are we :
Speak ! dost thou know the fair Walborg?
    Hath she forgotten me ?"

" Fair Walborg is a maiden sweet !
    I ken her certainlie ;
Many a knight's son, pale wi' love,
    Doth woo her on his knee.

" Full oft fair Walborg have I seen,
    All in her sable gear !
The Court holds many a bonnie maid,
    But none can be her peer.

" And she is now a woman grown,
    A lily white and tall ;
Ah ! many a beauty lights the land,
    But she is crown of all !

" Dame Juliet sleeps 'neath kirkyard stone,
    By her proud husband's side :
Queen Malfred fostered Walborg well,
    When her dear mother died.

" And gold is on her small white hand,
    And pearls are in her hair ;
Yet is she named Sir Axel's bride
    By people everywhere.

" They call her Axel's own true-love,
    Yet loveless is her lot ;
They seek her for Prince Hogen's bed,
    And murmur, and scheme, and plot."

It was Sir Axel Thorsen drew
    His cloak across his face,
And stept before the Emperor
    All in the audience-place.

" All hail to thee, my Emperor !
    Thou art my lord and pride,
And on my knee I crave thy leave
    To fatherland to ride.

" For strange men seek my goods and gear,
　　Now father and mother are dead ;
But most I fear for my own true-love,
　　Whom others seek to wed."

" Leave shalt thou have right willingly,
　　Herewith I give it thee ;
And till thou dost return again,
　　Thy place shall open be."

With armèd men from the Emperor's Court
　　Doth Axel Thorsen hie,
And all the Emperor's courtiers bid
　　" Good speed," as he rides by.

With thirty armèd men behind,
　　So swiftly did he ride,
That when he reached his mother's gate
　　Not one rode at his side.

Up to his mother's castle gate
　　Rode Axel, gloomy and grim ;
There stood Helfred his sister sweet,
　　Who soothly greeted him.

" Thou standest here, my sister sweet,
    Nor thought me close at hand !
How fares Walborg, mine own true-love,
    The rose of all the land ?"

" With that sweet May it fareth well,
    For great hath been her gain—
She is the Queen's own waiting-maid,
    And bonniest of the train."

" Thy counsel, sister, give to me,
    As tender sisters can :
How may I speak with my true-love,
    Unheard by mortal man ?"

" Go, dress thyself in beauteous silk,
    In silk and eke in fur ;
Say that thou carriest from me
    A message unto her."

III. THE RE-MEETING.

It was Sir Axel Thorsen
    Unto the Court hied he,
And as they came from vespers, met
    The maiden companie.
The wheel of Fortune goes round and round.

He touched sweet Walborg's white, white hand,
    And soft and low he said,
" I am a trusty messenger
    From the fair dame, Helfred."

She brake the seal, and on her knee
    Spread smoothly out the screed,
And there were words but one could write
    For only one to read.

There lay five rings of red, red gold,
    Enwrought with lily and rose.
" Walborg, thine own betrothen knight,
    Sir Axel, sends thee those.

" Thou vowed to be his own true-love,
    And wilt not break thy vow :
I loved thee when thou wert a child,
    And dearly love thee now."

There on the castle balcony,
    By earth and heaven above,
By everything that solemn is,
    They sware a vow of love :

By Mary Mother did they sware,
    And by Saint Dorothy,
In honour would they live and love,
    And eke in honour die.

Sir Axel rode to the Emperor's Court
    As blithe as well could be ;
Maid Walborg in the high chamber
    Sat laughing merrilie.

—

For months full five they dwelt apart,
    And months full nine thereto :
Eleven earls' sons at Walborg's feet
    Kneel down, and plead, and sue.
The Wheel of Fortune goes round and round.

    Eleven fair and gallant knights
        Knelt down, and prayed, and sued ;
    And twelfth the proud Prince Hogen came
        And early and late he wooed.

" Hearken to me, O sweet Walborg !
    O Walborg, turn and hear ;
Thou shalt be Queen and wear the crown,
    An thou wilt be my dear ! "

" Hearken to me, Prince Hogen,
    It is vain to plead and sue ;
Sir Axel hath my love and truth,
    And I will aye be true."

Wroth grew the young Prince Hogen,—
    Drew his cloak across his face,
And hied unto his mother dear
    All in the audience-place.

" Hail unto thee, dear mother mine !
    Thy counsel give to me !
I seek to wive the May Walborg,—
    She answereth scornfullie !

" In honour and truth I sue and woo,
    Offering riches and land ;
She cries Sir Axel is her dear,
    And he shall have her hand."

" If May Walborg her troth hath given,
    Then is she vowed and won,
And many a May as sweet as she
    Bides in the Court, my Son."

" Full many a May is at the Court,
    But none so high in grace ;
Full many a noble May I ken,
    Yet none so fair of face."

" Thou canst not win the maid by force,—
        That were a shame and woe ;
    Thou hast a sword, but he she loves
        Can wield a sword alsò ! "

    More wroth grows young Prince Hogen,
        And from the palace flies,
    And meeteth Knud, the Black Friàr,
        With coal black hair and eyes.

" Why paceth my lord so sadly forth,
        With dull and heavy gait ?
    If aught hath happ'd to cause him woe,
        Let him unfold it straight."

" A grievous woe hath happ'd to me,
        A sorrow sore to tell :
    The fair Walborg betrothen is
        Unto the young Axèl."

" Ne'er shall he bear the maiden home,
        Though they betrothen be,
    For in our cloister black we keep
        May Walborg's pedigree :

" And they are born of two sisters,
  Full stately dames and fair,
 And one nurse held both lass and lad
  When they baptizèd were.

 Thence brethren by the cloister law
  They are full certainlie,
 Thence can we prove them lass and lad
  Akin in fourth degree.

" To chapter summon priests and clerks,
  And they shall swift decide :
 Sir Axel by the cloister black
  Shall lose his lily bride ! "

V. THE CHURCH DISSOLVES THE BETROTHAL.

 It was the young Prince Hogen
  Spake to his trusty groom :
" Go, summon Walborg's uncles straight
  Into the audience-room."
The Wheel of Fortune goes round and round.

The earls around the broad board stand
　　And the great chamber fill :
" Our noble lord hath sent for us,
　　And we would hear his will."

" Your bonnie niece, the sweet Walborg,
　　In honour I crave of ye,
And surely if ye will consent,
　　The May my Queen shall be."

Answered the maiden's uncles three,
　　And their delight was great,
" Thus to be sought by the prince himself,
　　Sooth, she is fortunate !"

It was the noble uncles wrapt
　　Their faces in mantles red,
And strode into the high chamber
　　Before the Queen, Malfred.

And first they hailed the comely Queen,
　　And wished her right good cheer,
And then they hailed the sweet Walborg,
　　Who waited trembling near.

" Hail unto thee, O bonnie niece !
    Fair may thy fortune be !
If thou wilt take the fair young prince
    Whom we would wed to thee."

" And have ye falsely promised me ?
    Then hearken what I say,—
To Axel, to my dearest dear,
    I will be true for aye."

Then answered back her uncles three,
    Those mighty earls and bold,
" Never, in sooth, thou wilful girl,
    Shalt thou that troth-plight hold."

It was the young Prince Hogen,
    He hastily wrote again,
And summonèd the archbishop,
    With his clerks seven times ten.

It was Erland the archbishòp,
    He read in angry mood,
" Shame on the planner of this deed,
    Ay, first and last, on Knud !"

Proud Erland stood before the board,
    And spake full calm and clear :
" My honoured lord hath sent for me,
    And humbly wait I here."

" I have a bonnie maiden wooed,
    Whom thou shalt make my bride :
Dear is Sir Axel to her heart,
    But he must stand aside."

They wrote the solemn summons out,
    They read it out in state,—
It called the lovers to appear
    Before old Erland straight.

The matin-song was sounding,
    All in the morning tide—
To kirk, and with his own true-love,
    Must young Sir Axel ride.

The knight he climbs upon his steed,
    And sighs to hear the bell ;
The May rides in her coach behind,
    And hides her sorrow well.

The knight hangs o'er his saddle-bow,—
   His thoughts they wander wide;
The May rides in her coach behind,
   And hides her pain by pride.

Without the Kirk of our Ladye
   They all from horse alight,—
Into the holy kirk there steps
   Full many a gallant knight.

There in the aisle are the lovers met
   By the bishop and his clerks,
And woefully their faces look,
   To every eye that marks.

There meeteth them the archbishop
   Holding his silver wand,
And round about with gloomy looks
   The Black Friar brethren stand.

Then forth stept Knud the Black Friar,
   The convent book gript he,
And read that Axel and Walborg
   Were kin in fourth degree.

The record old of the convent cold
    He read full loud and slow ;
Akin were they by rite of kirk,
    Akin by birth alsò.

Cousins by birth they surely were
    In fourth degree akin ;
For such to wed, the grim law said,
    Were little else than sin.

They both were born of Gildish race,
    Akin in fourth degree :
Sir Axel and the fair Walborg
    Must never mated be.

" One nurse held both unto the font
    When they were baptizèd ;
Sir Asbiorn sponsor was to both,"
    The ghostly record said.

Yea, kin they were by birth and blood,
    And kin by ghostly rite,—
The kirk forbade that such a pair
    In honour should unite.

Up to the altar they were led,
　　Weary and pale of hue :
They placed a kerchief in their hands,
　　And, praying, cut it in two.

They placed the kerchief in their hands,
　　And cut it cruellie.
" The hand of Fate is stronger far
　　Than any folk that be.

" The kerchief ye have cut in two,
　　And still we hold the parts,
But never, never can ye cut
　　The love of leal young hearts."

They took the ring from her finger,
　　The bracelet from her hand,
They gave the knight his gifts again,
　　Breaking the true-love band.

Sir Axel on the altar cast
　　Bracelet and ring of gold,
And sware so long as he did live
　　His love should ne'er grow cold.

VI. PRINCE HOGEN IMPEACHES WALBORG'S PURITY.

Then wroth grew young Prince Hogen,
 Wrapt in his mantle red.
" If thou canst not forget her now,
 She is not pure !" he said.
The wheel of Fortune goes round and round.

Up spake the good old archbishop,
 All in his priestly guise,
" Who knoweth not the strength of love
 I hold to be unwise !

" Water may quench the flaming fire.
 Put out the brand ablaze,
But the fire of love in mortal breast
 No power of earth allays.

" Hot, hot is the summer sun,
 And who its heat can still ?
Hotter far is the fire of love,
 And it must cheer or kill."

Young Hogen spake to young Axèl
    Wrapt in his mantle red,
" This thing, I swear, shall have an end,
    Though I should die !" he said.

Wroth grew the young Prince Hogen,
    Treading the paven floor :
" To-morrow shalt thou swear an oath,
    Or rue thy baseness sore.

" To-morrow shalt thou swear an oath
    Upon thy sword and glaive,
That, falsely wooing fair Walborg,
    Thou ne'er hast played the knave."

" And must I swear upon my sword
    Walborg from stain is free ?
That will I do, and with my sword
    Uphold her purity !"

Sir Henrik's wife, Dame Eskelin,
    Awoke from sleep in fright :
" Saint Bridget clear unto my soul,
    What have I dreamt this night !

" I dreamt my cousin Juliet rose
    Out of the black, black grave,
And cravèd me full sisterlie
    Her child, Walborg, to save.

" Lord, I have seven sons, and each
    Hath thirty men beside—
Let them go bind the sword on thigh,
    And unto Walborg ride.

" Lord, saddle, saddle ten good steeds,
    And ride in lordly state ;
Follow thy sons ! stand by her side !
    It is not yet too late !

" Seven sons we now together have—
    Seven strong and goodly wights—
And it is now our hope and joy
    They hold themselves like knights.

" I and Dame Juliet alsò
    Were of two sisters born ;
And by this deed against Walborg
    We two are brought to scorn."

The sun is shining on the heath,
    All in the morning-tide,
As, bent to swear Walborg is pure,
    The gallant champions ride.

Sir Axel, all in armour clad,
    Reached out his hand, and cried,
" Welcome, ye knights of Gildish race,
    Right welcome, to my side ! "

The seven knights then forward strode
    Arrayed in sable all :
" We come to swear with Sir Axel,
    And with him stand or fall ! "

Then tears ran down the maiden's cheek
    Like rain, and she made moan :
" What men that be will swear by me ?—
    I am alone, alone ! "

Then answered back her uncles three,
    Those wroth and angry men,
" Thou hast loved alone—thou hast sworn alone—
    Thou canst swear alone again ! "

But murmured Erland, archbishòp,
　　With mild and gentle mien,
" Kinsmen thou hast full many here—
　　Friends only few, I ween.

" Kinsmen thou hast full many here,
　　Yet none to take thy part :
God help thee from thy peril now,
　　And soothe thy gentle heart ! "

" My father and my mother are dead,
　　And piteous is my plight ;
But God, who helpeth all in need,
　　Knows well my soul is white.

" Dame Juliet sleeps 'neath the marble stone,
　　Sir Immer in black, black clay ;
I should not stand alone and weep
　　Were they alive this day."

And while she sat in sorrow and fear,
　　Weeping and desolate,
She saw Sir Henrik riding swift
　　Up to the castle gate.

With hasty step he ran to her,
 And cheerfully he cried,
" Thou goest to take the oath, and I
 Will take it by thy side.

" Dame Eskelin, my own goodwife,
 Holdeth thine honour dear ;
Thy mother and she were kin by blood,
 And therefore am I here.

" Now, forward, forward, my seven sons,
 And swear the May is true ;
Seven sons of Carl from Sonderland
 Will do as we must do."

Seven earls' sons, in sable clad,
 Stept lightly forth to swear—
Full daintilie they all were clad,
 And curlèd was their hair.

Seven young counts stept forward next,
 And fair was each and bold,
Curled also was their golden hair ;
 Their swords were bright with gold.

" To swear the May is free from stain,
     Ho ! hand in hand come we :
Step forth and speak, O noble pair !
     For all shall hark to ye."

One hand upon the Mass-book laid,
     The other on his brand,
Sir Axel swears ; and, round about,
     His gallant kinsmen stand.

He held the sword-hilt in his hand,
     The blade upon a stone,
And there he swore the May was pure,
     And in no woman's tone.

" Dear, dear to me is May Walborg,
     That stainless May and meek,
Yet never have I been so bold
     As even to kiss her cheek ! "

She touched the Mass-book with her hand,
     Sware by our Lady of Grace,
" Mine eyes have scarcely been so bold
     As look into his face."

They raised bright banners o'er her head,
   And none her oath denied,
And they bare her along unto her bower,
   And called her "Prince's Bride."

Outspake young Prince Hogen
   Unto that gathering bright,
" Never a gentleman or squire
   Shall ride away this night."

He said, " The bonnie May Walborg
   I my Heart's Dearest hold,
And she shall be mine own sweet Queen,
   And wear the crown of gold."

VII. THE LAST FAREWELL.

The cloth was spread, the board was filled,
   The mead and wine ran free :
Sir Axel Thorsen sat apart,
   Beside his lost ladie.
The wheel of Fortune goes round and round.

" Speak to me, speak to me, Heart's Dearèst,
    While here we sit alone ;
  What peace remains on earth for me,
    What cheer for thee, mine own ?"

" If they should wed me to the King
    And crown my brow with gold,
  Although I live a thousand years,
    My love will ne'er grow cold.

" But I will gold embroidery sew,
    And moan for my true-love ;
  In lonely pain will I remain,
    Like to the turtle-dove :

" She sleepeth not in greenwood bough,
    She seeketh not to eat,
  She drinketh ne'er the pure clear well
    Till muddied with her feet.

" But thou, my lord, wilt gladly ride
    To hunt the forest hart ;
  If thoughts of me e'er trouble thee,
    Full soon they will depart.

" Ay, thou, my lord, wilt merrilie ride
    To chase the hind and hare ;
If thoughts of me e'er trouble thee,
    They will be light as air."

" And if I chase in greenwood grove
    To drown the thought of thee,
What shall I do at midnight hour
    When sleep comes not to me ?

" My lands and goods I straight will sell
    For pieces golden red,
And hie away to a strange countrie,
    And mourn till I be dead."

" Dear lord, sell not thy goods and lands
    For pieces golden red,
But hie away to old Asbiorn,
    And wive his child, Allhed.

" Hie there, and woo the fair Allhed,"
    The weeping Walborg cried,
" And I will take the mother's place.
    And sadly bless the bride."

"Never will I fair maiden woo,
    Never, ah, nevermore !
I will be leal, though I might wed
    The child of the Emperòr ! "

In stept Erland, archbishòp,
    And tapped their cheeks of snow :
" Now must ye say a sad ' good-night,'
    For it must e'en be so."

The archbishop raised up his hand,
    And angrily cried out,
" Shame be the fall of Black Friar Knud,
    Who brought this grief about ! "

Sir Axel bade the May good-night,
    And his voice was hoarse with pain,
His heart was aching with its woe
    Like a slave beneath his chain.

Fair Walborg hied to the high chamber,
    And her maidens followed slow,
Her heart was like the flaming fire,
    Her cheek was like the snow.

Early in the morning-tide,
    When sunshine 'gan to fall,
The gentle Queen arose from sleep,
    And called her maidens all.

Queen Malfred bade her maidens sweet
    To work the red, red gold ;
But still stood May Walborg, with heart
    As full as it could hold.

" Hearken, Walborg, bonnie May !
    Why stand so sad aside ?
Thy heart should happy be, because
    Thou art a prince's bride."

" Rather would I Sir Axel have,
    And love as poor folk may,
Than take the mighty gift ye bring—
    The crown of all Norwày.

" Ah, little care my kinsmen proud,
    But smile to find it so ;
My heart may bleed, my eyes may weep,
    My life may melt like snow !"

VIII. HOGEN AND AXEL FIGHT AGAINST THE ENEMY.

A gloomy time, two weary months,
    Passed bitterlie away :
Sir Axel and the fair Walborg
    Smiled neither night nor day.
The wheel of Fortune goes round and round.

Then came a war upon the land,
    And the foe rushed on in might ;
The young Prince Hogen verily
    Must lead his folk to fight.

Prince Hogen called his men to field,
    Yea, priests and clerks alsò.
Sir Axel was a gallant knight,
    And was not loath to go.

It was the young Prince Hogen
    Rode up and down the land,
And called unto him every man
    With strength to wield a brand.

He called upon him every man
  Who could a weapon wield,
And as a captain of the host
  Bids Axel hie afield.

Sir Axel's shield was blue and white,
  And terriblic it shone,
And all the warriors could see
  Two bleeding hearts thereon.

There riding forth afield they saw
  The foeman's armour glance :
In sooth, 't was bloody strife of men,
  And not a ladies' dance !

Sir Axel strikes for fatherland,
  His sword reeks hot and red :
They who come face to face with him
  Drop from their saddles, dead.

Full many a gallant gentleman
  By his strong hand doth bleed ;
The noble and the base alike
  He tramples 'neath his steed.

He slays the lords of Oppeland,
    Who ride on chargers tall ;
King Amund's sons fall by his hand,—
    Full gallant foemen all.

As thick as hay by peasants tost,
    The killing arrows fly ;
Prince Hogen drops upon the dust,
    And, wounded sore, must die.

It was the young Prince Hogen
    He dropt from his charger gray ;
Sir Axel to the prince's side
    Full swiftly cut his way.

" Hearken, Sir Axel Thorsen,—
    Avenge my death on the foe,
And thou shalt get my lands and crown,
    And May Walborg also."

" Terribly will I wreak thy death
    Upon the coward foe :
Though score on score encircle me,
    I 'll give them blow for blow."

Sir Axel seeks the thick o' the fight,
  With black and angry frown,
And every wight he meets in fight
  Is slain and trampled down.

So manfullie Sir Axel fought,
  No man his sword dared meet :
Swiftly he slew the gallant foe
  As a reaper reapeth wheat.

So manfullie Sir Axel fought,
  Till his armour stained the field,
So manfullie Sir Axel fought
  Till cloven was his shield ;

Still manfullie Sir Axel fought
  Until his helm was cleft ;
Yet manfullie Sir Axel fought
  Till his sword brake at the heft.

With eight red wounds upon his breast
  Sank Axel, worn and spent ;
Deeply he breathed, brightly he bled,
  As they bare him to his tent.

Ah ! woefully Sir Axel bled
　　After the victorie :
The latest words he spake alive
　　Were of his dear ladie :

" Say to my love a thousand ' good-nights ; '
　　Our Lord will soothe her pain :
In heaven above full speedilie
　　We two shall meet again ! "

IX. WALBORG HEARS THE FATAL NEWS.

In before the fair Queen's board
　　Sir Axel's page did walk ;
He was a wise and gentle child,
　　And fittingly could talk.
The wheel of Fortune goes round and round.

" Maidens, who sew the linen white
　　And eke the silk so red,
Prince Hogen and the young Axel
　　They both are lying dead.

" Dead is the young Prince Hogen,
 He lies on his bier of death !
Sir Axel to avenge his fall
 Fought till his dying breath.

" And they have won the victorie,
 And they for Norway died,
And many a knight lies dead afield,
 And many a swain beside."

Ah ! bitterlie Queen Malfred wept
 All for her gentle son ;
Sweet Walborg wrang her lily hands
 For her belovèd one.

May Walborg called her little page,
 And murmured woefullie,
" Haste ! haste, and find my chest of gold,
 And bring it in to me.

" Place my gray steed in the chariot red,—
 To cloister I 'll begone ;
I never can forget Axèl
 So long as I live on."

Without the Kirk of our Ladie
    She from her chariot stept,
And as she stept into the kirk
    Most bitterlie she wept.

She took the gold crown from her head,
    She set it on a stone.
" And never will I mate with man,
    But live a maid alone.

" Twice have I been a maid betrothed,
    But never yet a wife,
And now unto the cloister cold
    I give my woeful life."

X. WALBORG TAKES THE VEIL.

They brought to her the red, red gold
    That filled the golden chest,
She shared the same among the friends
    Who had been goodliest.
The wheel of Fortune goes round and round.

She took the great neck-band of gold,
    Inlaid with jewels fine,
And that, for having loved her long,
    She gave to Eskeline.

Unto Sir Henrick next she gave
    The great clasped armlet bright,
Because he sware with mouth and hand
    Her name and fame were white.

She took a hundred golden rings,
    And silver and gold good store,
And these she gave the gallant knights
    Who with Sir Henrick swore.

She dowered the kirk and cloister old,
    And priests and clerks so gray,
That they for Axel's soul and hers
    With daily Mass should pray.

She gave to widows and fatherless bairns,
    And footsore pilgrims old,
And to the image of Saint Ann
    She gave her crown of gold.

" Hither, hither, O archbishòp,
    Scatter me o'er with clay !
For here I take the cloister oath
    And quit the world for aye.

" Hither, hither, O archbishòp,
    And make me God's alone,
For ne'er shall I quit cloister more
    Till I be cold as stone."

Many and many a gallant knight
    Wept like a little child
To see them cast the black, black dust
    Over that maiden mild.

So sweet Walborg in cloister dwelt
    A weary nun for long,
And never missed the blessed Mass
    Or holy vesper-song.

Full many a noble woman and maid
    In cloister dwell, I wis,
But never a maiden of them all,
    So fair as Walborg is.

Far better never be born at all
　　Than wearily mourn and 'plain—
Than drink a bitter daily cup,
　　And eat the bread of pain.

God's ban be on the wicked churl,
　　And thriftless may he be,
Who tears in twain two lovers' hearts
　　That love so tenderlie !
The wheel of Fortune goes round and round.

THE BLUE COLOUR.

I LOVE you, Heaven's divinest blue !
　　The light I cannot reach unto ;
With earthly joys and wishes, I
Remain heart-laden utterly.

I love the shadowy blue of waves,
That whisper in the sweet sea-caves ;
But earth so pleasant is to me,
I would not sail upon the sea.

I love the blue of yonder plots,
Where blow the sweet forget-me-nots ;
But dare not pluck them from their bed,
They would so soon be vanishèd.

The blue for me—and here it lies,
Sweet-shining in my true-love's eyes,
Where flower's blue, heaven's blue, sea's blue
　　shine,
Mingled, to make my bliss divine

THE ROSE.

N the warmth of a singer's chamber, where
      never wild wind blew,
Whither no cold was wafted, a tender rose-tree grew.

The sweet wood sent out knots, and each a red rose
      gave :
And " My tree," cried the happy singer, " shall grow
      upon my grave ! "

Then came the Angel who smileth through tears
      while mourners weep,
And the tree was red and in bloom, but the singer
      was asleep.

And his friends fulfilled his wish : the tree grew
      over the dead ;
The sunrise shimmered upon it, and the sunset
      stained it red.

L

But the cold, cold winds of night blew in the leaves
　　　of the tree ;
Alas ! 'twas born for a chamber, not for the life of
　　　the free.

Poor tree ! in the air of freedom thou couldst not
　　　live and grow,
Whence over thy grave, poor singer ! not one of thy
　　　roses blow !

LITTLE CHRISTINA'S DANCE.

"LITTLE CHRISTINA, come dance with me,
  Hither unto me !
And a silken sark will I give to thee."
For methought that no one knew me !

" A silken sark is a precious thing,
  But I would not dance for the son of a King."

" Little Christina, come dance with me—
  Two silver shoes shall thy guerdon be."

"Two silver shoes were a guerdon fair,
  But I would not dance with the King's own heir."

" Little Christina, come dance with me,
  And a red gold band I will give to thee."

" A red gold band is a precious thing,
  But I would not dance for the son of the King."

"Little Christina, come dance with me,
  And half a gold ring shall thy guerdon be."

"I dance not for half of golden ring—
  I would not dance with the son of the King."

"Little Christina, come dance with me—
  Two silver knives will I give to thee."

"Two silver knives were a guerdon fair—
  But I would not dance with the King's own heir."

"Little Christina, come dance with me,
  And my honour and troth I will plight to thee." *

  Into his arms leapt the little one fair—
  The pale, pale face set in golden hair.

  Round and round the dancers sped,
  Till the cheeks of Christina were rosy red.

"My troth and plight I have given to thee"—
  They are wedded together where none can see.

* This plighting of troth was, as nearly as possible, equi-valent to marriage.

The days and the nights have swiftly flown :
Little Christina is all alone.

On a mantle spread in a secret place,
Christina lies with a blush on her face.

To the King on his throne a murmur runs—
" Little Christina hath two little sons."

Lonely little Christina lies :
There is royal light in her little ones' eyes.

The monarch stands by the maiden's bed,—
He covers his face and bows his head :

He covers his face with his mantle blue :
" Name me the sire of thy children two."

" Now God the Father forgive my shame !
Be he living or dead, I know not his name.

" My father wandered the ocean o'er ;
He built me a bower on the ocean shore.

" Thither came men of the stormy sea,
With dancing and feasting and melody ;

" Thither came men of the stormy sea,
  Each of them seeking to marry me.

" With none of them danced I night or day,
  No man of them stole my heart away.

" A stranger plighted his troth to me—
  We were wedded together where none could see."

" Hearken, little Christina, to me :
  What gifts did the stranger give to thee ? "

" He gave me a sark of the silk so fine,—
  It covers this beating heart of mine ;

" He gave me shoes of the silver bright,—
  They are worn with seeking him day and night :

" He gave me a band of the red, red gold,—
  It burns like fire on my temples cold ;

" He gave me the half of a golden ring,—
  Shame and pain may the other half bring !

" He gave me two silver knives of price,—
  Would they were stuck in his heart of ice ! "

The monarch trembled and tried to speak,
Then plucked the mantle of blue from his cheek.

" O little Christina ! my sweet ! my true !
I am the sire of thy children two !

" O little Christina ! my sweet ! my true !
That dance of thine thou shalt never rue !"

He clasps in his arms the little one fair,
The pale, pale face set in golden hair.

The rumour wanders from town to town—
She is Queen Christina, and wears a crown !

Little Christina is throned in pride—
    Hither unto me !
She sits by the King of Denmark's side.
    For I thought that no one knew me !

THE TREASURE-SEEKER.

WHILE the white snows are falling
    So glistening and cold,
And while the chilly tempest
    Shrieks in the wintry wold,
Safe in the chimney corner,
    With faces brown uplit,
Talking of village wonders,
    The quiet cotters sit.

And gray old Hans sits talking
    In the bright oven's light—
What would one hark to sooner
    Than tales he tells to-night?
" But is it true, then, father,
    That underneath the ground,
If men will seek them rightly,
    Such treasures may be found?"

" Ay, boy ! when the cock croweth
    One find the treasure may,
But if a word be spoken,
    It vanisheth away ! "
By strange wild thoughts kept silent,
    They gather, wondering-eyed,
When, lo ! there comes a knocking,
    And the door is opened wide ;

And bearing spade on shoulder
    Enters a peasant boy,
And though his face be haggard,
    He smiles as if with joy ;
His hair about his forehead
    By the wild wind is blown ;
And glancing round, he speaketh
    In words of eldritch tone.

" Chill, chill is all without there !
    And I am stiff with cold !
Hark ! hear the wild wind beating
    Upon the kirkyard old !
Deep was the treasure buried !
    Hard was the prize to win !
It lieth close without there--
    Help me to bear it in ! "

Bloody and pale he standeth,
    Trembling the cotters see—
" Art *thou* a treasure-seeker ? "
    He smileth craftilie.
Up in the air he springeth,
    Then standeth still once more,
And wipes his eyes a-weeping,
    And moveth to the door.

" Follow ! " he crieth, showing
    The spade begrimed with clay :
All trembling, hoping, follow,
    And mutter on the way.
And suddenly he halteth
    While midnight hour is tolled,
Where the dead lie a-sleeping,
    All in the kirkyard cold.

In the chill mist of midnight
    His lantern glimmereth dim ;
He entereth at the wicket,—
    Trembling they follow him.
Dark, dark is all around them,
    Loudly the wild winds rave,
And the lantern gleameth faintly
    Upon an open grave.

Nearer they creep, and nearer,
   Through the chill mist of night,
And look upon the treasure
   In the faintly glimmering light :
While thin sick beams are falling,
   Below them they behold
A black and blood-stained coffin,
   Half dug from the black mould.

" See !" cried the stripling, pointing,
   With wild and hollow eyes,
" Here in the grave's embraces
   My dearest treasure lies !
Four hours my hands have laboured
   Out in the tempest drear.
I bleed ! the clock is sounding !
   Eliza, I am here !"

" O God that art in heaven !
   This is the hapless lad
Who, when his true-love perished,
   For woe of heart grew mad ;
And from his home out creeping
   He here this night hath hied "—
Thus, tremblingly and faintly,
   The pale-faced cotters cried.

" See ! see how still he lieth
      In the coffin's cold embrace !
  Hark to the death-clock singing !
      God on his soul have grace !
  Raise him, and bear him homeward,"
      The shivering cotters said :
  They raised him from the coffin,
      He smiled—and he was dead !

SIGNE AT THE WAKE.

IT is wake to-night, it is wake to-night!
    Come, dance who will!
So many are dancing by candle-light.
Thither, alas! goes Signelil.

Fair Signelil to her mother spake,
" Mother, dear, may I see the wake?"

" What wouldst thou there, O little one?
    Sisters or brothers thou hast none.

" If thou alone to the wake-room go,
    Thine will be bitterness and woe.

" There dance the King and his companie:
    List to my rede and stay with me."

" The Queen and her maidens are also there,
    And I long to chat with those maidens fair."

So long the maiden prayed and cried,
    At last the mother no more denied.

" Go then, go then, if thou must, my child,
  But thy mother ne'er went to a place so wild."

Alone she went through the greenwood gloom
Unto the merry dancing-room.

As o'er the dusky meads she sped,
The Queen and her maidens had gone to bed.

Into the wake-room Signe tript ;
Wildly the dancers twirled and skipt—

Madder dance could never be ;
And the King danced there with his companie.

The King stretched out his hand in glee,
" Pretty maiden, come dance with me ! "

" Over the dale have I come to see
The Danish Queen and her companie."

" Dance with me and my merry men—
The Queen will soon be here again."

Light and lithe as a willow wand
She danced, and the monarch held her hand.

" Signelil, pause on thy small white feet ;
Sing me a song of love, my sweet ! "

" I know no love-song, sad or gay,
    But I will sing ye the best I may."

Sweet she sang : the King stood nigh ;
    The pale Queen heard in her chamber high.

The pale Queen heard upon her bed :
" Which of my maidens sings ? " she said.

" Who dares to linger after me,
    And sing so loud to that companie ? "

Answered the page in kirtle red,
" 'Tis none of thy maidens who sing," he said ;

" None of thy maidens linger still ;
    'Tis the little peasant, Signelil."

" My cloak and hood come give to me ;
    I am fain this maiden's face to see."

Better dance could never be ;
    And the King danced there with his companie.

Round and round in a ring went they :
    The Queen stole down and watched the play.

" Sin and sorrow ! " thought the Queen,
" That he holds the hand of one so mean ! "

The pale Queen whispered quietlie,
" A wine-filled beaker bring to me."

The King reached out his hand : " Sophiè,
Hither, and trip a step with me."

" I will not dance till this maiden fine
Drinketh to me in the red, red wine."

Signelil drank the wine so red,—
On the floor of the hall she lieth dead !

Long looked the King on that maiden sweet,
Slain so cruelly at his feet.

" I have never, since I drew breath,
Known sweeter maid or fouler death."

Maids and good women wept full sore
As they followed the corse through the kirkyard
door.

There ne'er had been so black a deed,
Come, dance who will !
Had Signe hearked to her mother's rede.
Thither, alas ! goes Signelil.

BALLANTYNE AND COMPANY, PRINTERS, EDINBURGH.

www.ingramcontent.com/pod-product-compliance
Lightning Source LLC
Chambersburg PA
CBHW031104020726
47495CB00007B/2041